THE SINNERS OF ERSPIA

"Where are we going?"

"To my ship."

"Ship?" The word was strange to her. "What's that?"

He didn't answer.

"That man," she said a few yards on, "why does Drosh call him master?"

"They all do. He is the High Priest of the Forces of Darkness."

She was quick to catch the personal pronoun. "They? Don't you, then?"

"No."

"Why not?"

"Because I don't come from here. I'm from another world."

"Another world?" She slowed down, puzzled. "I didn't know there was another world."

Laedo barked a harsh laugh. "Don't you know what this place is, you little fool? This Erspia, as you call it? It isn't a world at all, in the proper sense. It's a planetoid, no more than thirty or forty miles in diameter, with a gravity generator in the centre. It's a set-up."

Fiction by Barrington Bayley

THE SINNERS OF ERSPIA

Barrington Bayley

Cosmos Books

THE SINNERS OF ERSPIA

Cosmos Books is an imprint of
Wildside Press
PO Box 301
Holicong, PA 18928-0301
www.wildsidepress.com

For more information, contact Wildside Press.

ISBN: 1-58715-511-7

ONE

The Sinners

Histrina scarcely dared raise her head once she was in the chapel. Eyes downcast, she followed the tonsured acolyte across the tiled floor, walking between slanting slats of hard white light which entered through narrow openings high in the walls. They were like arrows picking out stone recesses and elaborate wood carvings in the cool, otherwise dim place of worship. She passed before the altar upon which a small flame burned in front of a polished stone figure, automatically pausing to press the back of her hand to her forehead in the traditional sign of submission to the Good Lord.

Then she came to the little confessional room where the priest was waiting. The acolyte disappeared through the drapes, returning after a moment. Punctiliously he folded his hands. "The Father will see you now, my child."

Her heart beating wildly, she went in. Sitting in an ornate upright chair, wearing a maroon cope, the Father smiled at her kindly, the wrinkles of his benign face creasing.

She obeyed as he motioned her to kneel on the cushion before him. The small room seemed to enclose them both as if nothing else existed in the whole of Erspia. Only the cheep of a bird somewhere outside broke the heavy silence. There were no windows. Light came from an oil lamp on the nearby table. Clenching her hands together, she tried to avoid looking directly at the Father's large polished boot. She felt utterly in his power.

The Father sighed and then uttered a brief recitation. "*Heerwecumlord*, lighten us our bodily burdens." He sighed again. "So why are you here, daughter?"

The question was ritualistic. "To accuse myself, Father."

"And of what do you accuse yourself?"

"I—" She swallowed. "I have been having thoughts, Father."

"Tempting thoughts?"

"Yes, Father."

"The Evil One sends bad thoughts to us all, my child. You have been taught how to resist them."

"I don't think I can resist them much longer, Father." Her words came out abjectly. "They are too strong."

"What is it the Evil One is trying to make you do, child? Hurt someone?"

"No . . . well, yes, sometimes he tries to make me do that. But I can resist that by concentrating on good thoughts, as we are taught. This is something else. Feelings that keep making me want to—to—"

The priest leaned forward, almost eagerly. "Yes, daughter?"

"There is a young man, Father," she said demurely. "I keep wanting to . . . do sinful things with him."

The priest leaned back, sighing again and tutting to himself. "All is clear. This is the Evil One's most powerful weapon. The body itself collaborates with it, for the body is full of darkness and corruption."

Her voice was a whisper. "What can I do, Father?"

"The Lord will help you to fight these thoughts."

"But it is so difficult, Father. They are so overwhelming. Especially when night comes—"

"Yes, the Evil One is stronger at night. Stronger than the Lord himself at times. But he must be fought. If you but once give way to the lecherous thoughts he puts in your head, you will instantly be his. He will force you to do other things as well—steal, murder, lie. He will banish all the good and clean thoughts that the Lord sends to you, and your life will be one of wretchedness and crime."

"Yes, Father. But help me—help me to be strong."

The priest's voice became stern. "You can help yourself, my child. When the Evil One's fever comes over you, when you imagine that you can resist no longer—and you must believe me when I tell you that you always *can* resist longer—then call on the Lord by his secret name." He leaned forward again, placing his hand on her bowed head. "I am instructing you in this because you are obviously in danger. You were told this name when you were confirmed in the ways of the Lord. Can you remember it?"

"Name, Father?"

"Yes." His lips brushed close to her ear. *"Ormazd!"* he hissed. "Call on Ormazd in your time of strife. He will hear you."

"But is that certain, Father?"

"Nothing is certain, my child," the priest answered sadly. "The Lord and the Evil One both struggle for our souls. Who wins depends on what we love most. But you must pray—pray to Ormazd, the sacred name of God the Good. Pray tonight and every night, when temptation comes in the dark hours."

She felt both his hands pressing down on her scalp as he mumbled a blessing. He signed for her to go. She pulled open the wood-panel door, pressed through the drapes and found the acolyte standing outside. Histrina had arrived specially early. Others from the village were beginning to file into the chapel now, forming a queue outside the confession rooms. She stepped silently past them, not meeting their eyes.

Outside, she realized she felt strengthened a little. Tomorrow she would be at confessional again, and the priest would ask her how she had fared during the night.

Oh, how would any of them ever be able to keep the Lord's way were it not for these daily sessions of advice and encouragement? Without the church, she was certain she would have fallen into the torments of sin long ago.

Yet for all that, this was the first time she had dared to confess the yearnings for lechery that of late had been stealing over her.

The small, bright sun was no larger in the sky than a peppercorn, and was dipping down towards the sharp edge of the horizon. On Erspia it was never possible to see very far. One could walk to any point on the horizon in a matter of minutes. To the eye it was as if the world were no more than a shelf of rock and soil that the sun was about to slip under.

Histrina, however, had never known any other world. To her this close little scene had the homeliness of normality. Night approached and birds were twittering, flying to their nesting places in the trees. She quickened her step to retrace her path to the village.

The road wound between stone-roofed cottages. An unexpected silence greeted her as she lifted the doorlatch to her parents' house. No one was there. They must be at confession, she thought. I must have missed them on the way. Oddly, she had thought they had already gone that afternoon.

Then, on the kitchen table, she found a note. *Have gone to see the Arrands' new baby. Won't be back till late.*

Unaccountably her heart sank. Somehow she didn't went to be alone in the house during the long evening.

With an abruptness that she had begun to find frightening, the sun winked below the horizon. Darkness began.

Already, it seemed in her imagination, urges were beginning to well up in her. She lit the lamp in the living room, then knelt before the family shrine, and prayed.

"Good Lord," she whispered, "deliver me from these unclean thoughts. Let my liking for Hugger be pure and friendly. I don't went to dwell on his body like this, O Ormazd."

She heard a noise, and gasped. But it was only a knock on the door. Rising, she went to open it. A handsome, smiling young man stood there. He wore a jaunty hat with a feather in it, and newly pressed shirt and breeches. In his right hand was a lance, which he leaned against the wall.

"Hugger!" she nearly shrieked.

Still smiling, he placed one foot in the door. "Aren't you going to let me in?"

Limply her hand fell from the latch and he was in, closing the door behind him. He extended a hand. "The kitchen is no place to talk. Shouldn't we go into the living room?"

"I suppose so. But you shouldn't be here. My parents are out."

"Yes, I know. I saw them going towards the Arrands."

It distressed her that he should come here and find her alone, but it was a distress that was rapidly turning to excitement. She led him into the living room, where she immediately set herself down before the shrine and began to pray once more, silently and intently, with eyes closed.

At length she rose. Hugger was pacing the room restively.

"Why do you have your lance with you?" she asked shyly.

"I've been exercising with the troop. Have to stay in shape if we're to keep the Evil One's horde away, eh? They say it's been growing in numbers lately."

"Yes."

She faced him, the lamplight falling on her pale features

and making them seem as though made of porcelain. His eyes wandered down the curves of her body, discernible through her loose gown, which showed off her shapeliness most fetchingly.

"You're looking nice," he said gruffly. He stepped closer, put his hand on her plump arm, then suddenly caught her up and pressed her to him to give her a lingering kiss. She went limp in his arms while the kiss lasted, afterwards turning her head aside, breathing heavily.

"That's—enough. No more."

He held her as she tried to pull loose. "Do you remember the day before last, in the field?" he murmured breathlessly in her ear. "When we nearly . . ."

"No! Don't speak of it!" In desperation she tore herself free. "We mustn't even think such wickedness!"

She was flushed. She had felt his swollen manhood pressing against her belly when he held her. In the field—Oh Ormazd help her!—her hand had nearly . . .

"If we were married it wouldn't be wicked," he said slyly. "So why is it wicked now?"

"You know very well! If we were married we would be consecrated by the Lord. Even then, it is sinful to be too much taken up with—with—"

"With lechery."

She nodded. Her flush turned deeper, became a blush.

Then she turned suddenly to confront him. "Have you been to confession today?"

His eyes dropped. He looked embarrassed.

"Oh, but you *must* go to confession every day!" Her eyes opened wide in dismay. "Nothing else can save you!"

"Well, I *haven't!*" With an almost savage movement he stepped towards her again. She tried to retreat but her back was to the sideboard. He put his hands behind her shoulders and buried his face in her hair. "I didn't dare tell the priest what's on my mind," he murmured. "You're so lovely, Histrina. You drive me mad. And I know you feel the same." His hands were hot, and they started wandering down her back, massaging her buttocks, coming round and up to squeeze her breasts.

She pushed at him, but her arms felt weak. "No! Stop that, Hugger!"

Now his breathing was so deep that she knew he was depraved. But that was not what was worrying her. What was worrying her most was that her heart was beating so loudly that it pounded in her eardrums and filled the whole room. She felt sure that he could hear this pounding as clearly as she could, and the knowledge embarrassed her.

He growled something incoherent as he dragged her away from the sideboard and forced her down on the couch. She squealed and struggled, but for the moment she forgot to call on the Lord.

Then her gown came up and she knew she was bared to him. He was staring avidly at her naked loins, while the tide of desire that surged through her drove her wild.

"No!" she cried. "No! Oh Ormazd! Ormazd! Don't let it happen! *Stop me from doing it!*"

But she *was* doing it, for Hugger tore down his breeches, threw himself on her, and she felt him entering her. He went in with only a prick of pain, for she was wet with excitement, and soon a sort of motion began in which both of them were rocking to and fro and thrusting against one another. And it was the sweetest, most delicious thing she had ever imagined, which she could no more stop than she could have stopped the setting of the sun, for all that she wept the whole time and never ceased shrieking the name of Ormazd.

Then even that, the secret name of the Lord, became an agonised croak in her throat while an explosion of pure pleasure drenched her from top to toe.

They lay limply, but only for a short while—was it minutes or seconds? Their corrupted bodies had not finished sating themselves with each other. They started again, and this time it lasted longer, and the explosion when it came was of an even greater, more searing intensity.

They subsided. Histrina lay without an ounce of strength in her, whimpering with mortification.

She had *done it!* She had succumbed to the Evil One!

She sat up, drawing her knees to her chest and pulling her gown over herself as soon as Hugger got up from her. He rearranged his breeches. They looked at one another. Both were stricken.

A quavering groan escaped her lips.

Hugger slumped onto a chair near the table. He bowed his head. "You may as well know it," he said woodenly. "Why I didn't go to confession today. I haven't been these three days past. I have abandoned the Good Lord. I have been won over by Ahriman."

She put her hand to her mouth. "You spoke his secret name!"

"Like all his true followers."

"But how *could* you let yourself—"

"The same way *you* have!" he said angrily. "This is how it happens!"

"You forced me—"

"No, I didn't. You lusted for it, and you gave way to that lust. You could have stopped me but for that."

He stood and paced the room, just as he had before throwing himself on her. "Three nights ago I knew I was lost to Ormazd. Yes, the priest told me to use *his* secret name to fight temptation. Did he tell you the same?"

She nodded dismally.

"It didn't work, did it? Well, they say nothing is certain while Ahriman performs his work in the world. Ahriman won me."

"Didn't you fight him?"

"Of course!" Hugger's face blazed. "But when temptation gets stronger and stronger there comes a point where you *want* only bad thoughts. That's when Ahriman has you. You revel in what's bad. Good thoughts fade and seem silly. After that, there's no going back."

He stopped pacing and pulled her roughly up from the couch. "You too! You've done it now. There's no going back."

"We must try to find forgiveness!"

He shook his head wryly. "The priests won't help us with that. It would only encourage others. You know what will happen to us. We've fallen from grace and disobeyed the Lord's commandment. At the very least we'll be excommunicated and banished, perhaps imprisoned or even executed."

"Let's not let anyone know what we did! We can keep it secret."

"From Ormazd?" Hugger smiled. "Anyway, how do you suppose you can keep anything from the priests? They're experts. You'll be found out the next time you walk into a confessional."

"Then I don't know what we can do."

"There is only one thing. We must leave immediately, and never come back."

"Leave? But where can we go?"

He stared at her. "You know there is only one place. We belong to Ahriman now. We must join his horde."

"Oh, but my family, and everything! I can't leave them!"

"You have to leave them," Hugger said gruffly. "They'll throw you out anyway, once they know."

She started weeping openly then, not the hysterical crying of a few minutes previously, which was so bound up with pleasure and excitement, but a soft, quiet grieving.

"You did this to me," she sobbed.

"Yes, so I did." Hugger's eyes glittered with a perverted joy. "Now we can really enjoy ourselves . . . do anything we want." He started kneading her shoulders again, but then broke off abruptly.

"It will be a long journey. Get yourself a cloak. And one of your father's mantles for me."

"No! Please, we must think of something else."

As she would not stir, he went himself into the next room and poked about in a cupboard until he found what he wanted. He came back and draped the cloak about her. "Come on, I want to be well away from here before morning."

"You go," she sniffed. "I'm staying."

"I wouldn't leave you to face them all, Histrina. Besides—I want you with me."

He yanked her towards the door. She hesitated.

"Shouldn't we leave a letter?"

"No. They'd come after us. There's only one way to do it, and that's just to go and never think of them again!"

"Oh, my mother! My father!"

Still weeping, she allowed him to lead her outside, where he took up his lance.

"Be quiet!" he hissed. "Do you want the whole village to hear you?"

Histrina became compliant. They stole past the huddled houses of the village, from the chinks of whose shutters vagrant light gleamed. Beyond were the fields. These were eventually crossed, bringing the two fugitives to the thin soil and scrubland that covered most of Erspia.

She was not sure which feelings they were that made her obey him—fear of what would happen if she stayed, a lickerish anticipation of the delights she would experience by going with him, or simply abject acceptance that she was Ahriman's. All these feelings jostled within her as she left her lifetime home and set off across the narrow landscape.

The stars shone bright, casting a thin glow that made it possible to make out what was around them. The temperature had dropped but the air was not too chill; Histrina had never known it to get really cold since she had been born.

They said little during the journey. This was the first time she had wandered so far afield and there was, to be sure, a fascination in seeing parts of the world she had never set eyes on before. Not that Erspia seemed to change much as one moved across it. She was surprised, for instance, to find that the star patterns remained the same despite the distance that she and Hugger travelled. Surely things should look different if one saw them from a different angle? But all the stars did was move across the sky unchanging, just as they did at home.

For some hours they walked over the coarse grass and through soft, clinging bushes, and the night-time experience was so new to her that after a while she scarcely thought of what she was leaving behind. At about midnight Hugger called a halt for rest. They sank down on the turf. Histrina's feet ached.

"I wish we had brought something to eat and drink," she said.

Hugger grunted. Then he moved closer to her, until she fancied she could smell his masculine sweat. He put a hand on her thigh. "We'll feed on love," he said.

"Please, I'm tired," she said. "Besides, it isn't love. It's . . . Something else."

He leaned across and gave her a full, lingering kiss.

And it started all over again. The kissing, the fondling. Then a frenzied undressing until they were both naked under the starlight. Then their bodies, sliding, pressing and oscillating, all enveloped in a most delicious aroma of venery. Their scents mingled with that of the heathery turf and with the faint night breeze. She sighed, she moaned, she uttered insane little chuckles in her throat, and during the next hour and a half they found so many ways of gratifying themselves that it was as if they had been reborn into a new world.

Afterwards, when their bodies would respond no more, they lay on their backs and stared at the stars. "So," Hugger said dryly, "how do you like being evil?"

"Evil?" She tasted the word, as though savouring it. "Oh, Ormazd help me, but I love it!"

"Hmph. Ormazd. Ahriman. Let me tell you something, Histrina. I don't believe in either of them any more. It's all imagination. Something the priests thought up."

"But you *must* believe in them. Where else do our thoughts come from?"

"What makes you think they come from anywhere?"

"They must. They just seem to appear in our minds."

He was silent for a while. "Yes," he said then, "I can see how the idea must have arisen. Our minds are bombarded with thoughts and feelings all the time. So we have the Good Lord, Ormazd, to send us good thoughts, and the Evil One, Ahriman, who tries to overthrow him by sending us bad thoughts. But look up there, Histrina, into the sky. Do you see either Ormazd or Ahriman? I don't."

"They live among the stars."

"Where are they, then?"

"So how do we get our thoughts?"

"They come from inside us. They result from natural urges, just like being hungry or thirsty. That's all there is to it. There aren't any gods in the world. That's it."

He turned on his side, facing away from her, and picked idly at the grass. Histrina was shocked. She had heard of *atheism*. It was the greatest sin of all.

It was also the Evil One's greatest triumph. When a human being began to believe that there was no such thing as temptation, no such thing as the struggle of the gods, then he offered no resistance to that temptation.

She smiled mischievously to herself. Hugger was caught by Ahriman better than he knew!

Then she found herself drifting off to sleep.

Hugger was shaking her. She opened her eyes with a start.

The sun had risen, and its point-source shone just over the horizon. A warm breeze blew from it, making the bushes wave.

"Come on, we have to get going."

"I'm thirsty."

"So am I."

"We should have brought water," she complained, struggling to her feet.

"No, we shouldn't. I didn't bring any on purpose. We'd take our time if we had water. Your parents might be looking for us by now." He sounded annoyed. "We shouldn't have stopped!"

She was shivering; they had both slept naked. She picked at the untidy heap of her clothes and began getting into them. He watched her with interest, then started pulling on his own.

They set off again, in the direction of the sun. The ground was giving up its moisture in the new warmth of day, forming a faint mist just a foot or two deep. It was a familiar sight to them both. Often they had gone to work in the fields at dawn, striding through the transient haze.

On and on they toiled. At midday the heat was uncomfortable, and began to seem fierce, parched as they were. They trailed their mantles behind them. Histrina grew weary and depressed, thinking often of turning back for home, until Hugger nudged her with his elbow.

"Look."

A stream tinkled ahead of them. With a cry of delight Histrina quickened her pace, running ahead to throw herself down and cool her bare arms in the water, scooping it to her eager lips.

Hugger joined her and she heard him gulp greedily. When they had slaked their thirst she took off her sandals and dangled her feet in the running stream.

"Why is this the first water we've found? Does the world have so little of it, except at the village?"

"You don't see a stream unless you're right on top of it. We might have passed plenty."

She looked about them. Apart from the water the scenery was unchanged. "Where are we?"

"By now we must be almost a quarter of the way to the other side of Erspia."

"How far is it to the horde?"

Hugger shrugged. "They say the main camp is directly opposite the village. Right on the other side of the world."

"Oh no! You mean we have to go on like this for another four days?"

"I don't know. The horde moves about sometimes, attacking villages of the faithful. Perhaps we won't find it at all."

He splashed water on his face, wiping himself with the sleeve of his shirt. Histrina was staring across the stream. She pointed. "Over there," she said softly.

A horseman had appeared on the horizon. Evidently he had sighted them, for he was trotting swiftly onward, a lance held at his side.

Hugger quickly snatched up his own lance. The horseman came so close that he seemed to loom over them, before halting on the other bank.

Histrina stared fascinated at the apparition. The horseman wore a fantastic garb of many colours: a billowing cloak with strange designs on it, beneath that a glittering chemise that seemed to tumble and froth down his torso, and extraordinarily baggy breeks that were tied at the ankles. On his head was perched a wide-brimmed hat whose crown was a mass of coloured feathers.

The horse was clad, too, in a sweeping blanket or skirt that reached to its knees, while feathers sprouted from its neatly braided mane.

The horseman grinned at the pair. So far he had not threatened them with his lance, whose butt he rested against the ground. "What have we here? A pretty couple out walking where mother can't see 'em, eh?"

"Who are you?" Hugger demanded, gripping his lance nervously.

"Don't point your weapon at me, lad. I might get annoyed." The horseman nudged his mount suddenly and came splashing through the shallow water. On gaining the near bank he whirled his horse, forcing Hugger and Histrina apart. Hugger received a sharp rap on the skull with the butt of the horseman's lance, sending him reeling. At the same time Hugger's own lance was wrenched from his grasp and flung into the river.

The horseman dismounted, jabbing his own lance point

first into the turf and leaving it standing. Histrina shrank back as he approached her, still grinning.

"Where are you from, my dear? One of the villages?"

"Yes," she whispered. "Courhart."

"Courhart?" He frowned. "I know it, I think. You're some way from home, aren't you, my pretty? Come and let Drosh give you some home comforts. A spot of pleasure to cure your home-sickness."

He reached out, fondling her gown. Histrina gasped in alarm.

"You're a fine-looking one," he complimented. "One to be enjoyed."

Hugger, who had been on his knees, holding his head, was on his feet again. He took in the scene in an instant: the intruder, his back to him, pressing his attentions upon Histrina; the lance, carelessly left unguarded.

He stepped stealthily round the horse and pulled out the lance, but clumsily; 'Drosh' heard it rip turf, and turned unhurriedly, to see Hugger bearing down on him in an attempt to spit him.

Drosh did not seem in the least discommoded. He sidestepped, and in the same fluid motion drew a short sword which neither of the others had noticed beneath his cloak. Hugger was much too slow with the long lance. Drosh had turned inside his grip. The flat of his sword hit the villager's knuckles; at the same time his left hand seized the shaft of the lance and forced it up.

His sword blade plunged through Hugger's ribs.

It had all taken place in a second. Hugger uttered a choking sound and fell back. A sinister ecstatic look came to Drosh's face. He lifted his hand from the sword hilt and spread his fingers, letting the weapon fall with the corpse, hilt projecting skyward from the stilled chest.

Histrina screamed wildly. *"You've killed him!"*

"It's all in a day's work, my dear. I'll come to another bit of pleasantness shortly. It annoyed your friend to see me about to poke you, eh? Poked you often enough himself, I expect, has he?" While he spoke he picked up the lance which had slipped from Hugger's dead fingers. "A stiff young fellow, was he? Let's see him proud."

Hugger lay with legs outspread. Drosh chuckled savagely and drove the lance into the earth at his crotch, so that it thrust up as a longer companion to the upward slant of the sword, grotesquely suggestive.

Histrina was biting her knuckles. Her eyes stared. She stumbled back as Drosh came at her, but was too frightened to run. She screamed again, however, when he caught hold of her.

At first everything was a blur to her sensibilities. He was shoving her, forcing her down on her knees by the bank of the stream. Her face entered the water, was held there and held there. He was drowning her!

She gurgled, struggled feebly, and began to experience suffocation. Then the gown came up over her rump. She felt him enter her from behind, squirming to get himself firmly in.

He let her face out of the water when his thrusting motions became regular. It was like having Hugger in her, she realized, and the feelings were taking her over just as they had then. She began to moan, to wiggle, and when he saw that she was no longer resisting he let go her wrists, which he had held behind her back in one meaty hand, and there, her forearms in the mud, splashing in the water, they coupled and coupled.

When he had finished with her he stood up. She turned over and lay propped up on her elbows, all modesty gone, legs lewdly open. She merely avoided looking at the body of her former lover, even when Drosh put a foot on Hugger's chest and yanked his sword from the flesh with a sucking sound, wiping the blade on the dead man's shirt.

Oh, her experiences had come so fast in the past few hours, she realized!

And she had enjoyed them all! But now she became fearful that Drosh would kill her too. She need not have worried. He merely sheathed his sword and stood over her with a cheerful grin.

"So what were you doing out here, my lovely?"

Breathlessly, she answered. "We fell from grace. We were looking to join Ahriman's horde."

Drosh threw back his head. His strong white teeth flashed as he laughed. "Ahriman's horde! Well, you've found it!"

He held out his hand. "Come, lass, and welcome. But remember, you are Drosh's whore."

She accepted his hand and let him pull her to her feet. He went to his horse, put one foot in the stirrup, and was astride in one energetic leap. Then he helped Histrina to mount behind him, and reached over to recover his lance.

Histrina put her arms around his middle, resting her head on his shoulder, feeling the feathers of his hat tickle her hair. Drosh's heels kicked the horse's ribs. Together they went cantering swiftly across Erspia.

The rest of the day seemed to pass extraordinarily quickly, and so did the next night. Drosh explained that they were travelling counter to the sun's motion around the world, so that it seemed to move across the sky more rapidly than usual. Histrina could not understand any of this, but it was already night for the second time when they came to the Ahrimanic camp.

The sight that met her eyes, illuminated by starlight, by torchlight, and by the light of numerous campfires, was unlike anything she could have imagined.

Instead of the orderly, peaceful cottages of Courhart, there were gaily coloured tents. Instead of well-mannered folk, there were mobs that surged to and fro, drunkenly fighting and fornicating. The air of violence was thrilling. And the weapons! There was no one who was not armed!

Or no one who counted. Drosh guided his horse through the camp, picking his way through the jostling crowd. They passed by a fenced compound where men and women sat silently on the ground, passively watching the revels around them.

By the flickering firelight, Histrina suddenly recognised a face. She squealed, beating her fists on Drosh's back and begging him to halt. He reined in the horse, twisting round to see what had excited her.

"Borrow!"

The bearer of the name looked up, then when Drosh signed to him, rose to his feet and trudged to the fence, peering between the stakes.

"Borrow, I know you," she said. "You were taken by raiders from Courhart four years ago!"

He stared up at her. "I don't recognise you, lass, but it is as you say."

"What are you doing here?"

"The same as all do that are prisoners. We work the fields, growing food for the friends of the Evil One." He sounded subdued, beaten. There was no vestige of hope in his face.

Drosh laughed. "You see what a piece of luck you had in meeting me, girl! Do as you're told, or you too might end up in the compound."

The horse moved forward, leaving Borrow to turn away and resume his place on the cold earth. A snarling sort of music started up somewhere, a twanging of strings and the harsh bellow of some crude reed instrument. Seeing Borrow had momentarily saddened Histrina. Pangs of guilt rose in her; the camp faded before her eyes, and involuntarily she found herself thinking again of Courhart and of her family.

Then she thrust the thoughts from her mind and let her senses bathe in what was around her. They arrived before a tent larger than the others, before which two men sat at a large trestle table eating bread and meat and drinking from flagons constantly refilled by ragged girl servants.

Drosh and Histrina dismounted and Drosh tied his horse to a hitching post. He saluted the larger of the men at the table, who glanced up carelessly as he wiped meat juices from his plate with a piece of bread.

"So you're back, eh, Drosh? Well, what did you find?"

"Much as I hoped, master. Jong village is poorly defended. It's been too long since they were set upon, and they've grown careless."

"Good. We'll teach them a lesson in vigilance, then, eh? And have plenty of sport doing it." The man' s eye fell on Histrina. "What have you here? Is she from Jong?"

"No, master. She's from Courhart. I found her wandering. I sense she has a taste for our style of life."

The man Drosh had called 'master' rose and walked round the table. Histrina smelled sour wine on his breath as he stroked her smudged cheek.

He was a large, powerful man whose personal aura made him seem even more frightening than Drosh. Like everyone else in the camp he was flamboyantly garbed. She was dazzled by the gleaming-cloth-of-gold of his embroidered tunic.

"Courhart," he murmured, frowning. "It's right on the other side of Erspia—the furthermost of all the villages. Maybe we'll crush Courhart soon, my dear, and you can enjoy yourself torturing any you dislike there."

She shrank back, appalled by the thrill of anticipation the suggestion brought her. He caught hold of her by the throat, his huge hand squeezing her windpipe, and drew her close so that his face seemed to bulge.

"If you want to be one of us," he hissed, "you must worship Ahriman with all your heart. If he tells you to subject those who have displeased you to indignity, torture and death, you must do it with delight. If he tells you to do the same to those you once held dear, you must enjoy that, too."

He turned to the smaller man who still sat at the table, looking on expressionlessly. "Here, Laedo, you've proved uncommonly fastidious over our women so far. This one still seems to have scruples—maybe you'll like her."

He shoved Histrina forward. Drosh pursed his lips and caught the big man's eye.

"Oh come, Drosh, let's be generous. Give Laedo a little gift. I'll pay you for the girl. Tell you what, when we take Jong you can have first pick of all the women; select the five prettiest little wenches for yourself, how about that, eh?"

Drosh nodded. The master put a familiar arm around his shoulders. "Come and see what I've got lined up for tonight. It will amuse you."

The two wandered off. Histrina, her eyes demurely downcast, seated herself beside Laedo.

He was a sharp-faced man quite unlike any other she had ever seen. His nose was unusually thin, not flat and wide like most people's. His skin, too, was very pale, and the cast of his eyes was odd.

Still, he was not unattractive; but he seemed dour and uncomfortable, as if he didn't much like being where he was.

"I'm yours now,'" she said softly when he did not speak. She was uneasy at the readiness with which Drosh had dropped her. She realized that she needed *someone* to look after her.

A scream came from somewhere, ending in a note of choking agony. Laedo shuddered, and gulped down more wine as if it could shut off the sound.

"You're not mine," he said. "You can do as you like. You're free."

Histrina's face fell. She looked at the turmoil of the camp, wondering if she could make her way in it without being murdered or else consigned to the compound. Perhaps she would automatically be consigned there anyway, once she no longer had a protector.

"I don't *mind* being yours," she said in a small voice.

He grunted.

She said nothing for a while, and then an incident at the nearest campfire caught her attention. A fight had started up between two gaudily bedizened youths. A third joined in, quickly helping to subdue one of the others.

This unfortunate was then pushed towards the fire. His head was forced down to the flames and glowing embers. He shrieked as his hair and clothing caught fire and his flesh singed. Still they held him fast while his struggles grew ever more frantic and he was roasted alive.

No one around did anything to try to prevent it.

Histrina watched in fascination. Laedo groaned and staggered to his feet.

"I can't watch this. I'm off."

He loped swiftly round the tent and into the darkness. Histrina hesitated, then ran after him.

"Can't I come with you?" she called.

"If you like."

They were not far from the edge of the camp. The firelight grew dim and soon they were on untrodden turf. Still Laedo kept going, on into the night.

With difficulty she kept pace with him. He did nothing to acknowledge her, but neither, apparently, did he object to her presence.

"Where are we going?"

"To my ship."

"Ship?" The word was strange to her. "What's that?"

He didn't answer.

"That man," she said a few yards on, "why does Drosh call him master?"

"They all do. He is the High Priest of the Forces of Darkness."

She was quick to catch the personal pronoun. "They? Don't you, then?"

"No."

"Why not?"

"Because I don't come from here. I'm from another world."

"Another world?" She slowed down, puzzled. "I didn't know there was another world."

Laedo barked a harsh laugh. "Don't you know what this place is, you little fool? This Erspia, as you call it? It isn't a world at all, in the proper sense. It's a planetoid, no more than thirty or forty miles in diameter, with a gravity generator in the centre. It's a set-up."

His words made no more sense to her than had Drosh's explanation of the speeded-up days and nights. But now some sort of hump-formed building loomed out of the darkness, and Laedo was making for it. By the starlight she saw that it seemed to be made not of brick or timber, but of metal.

There was no ground-level door. Metal steps mounted about five feet, where there were the seams of a panel. Laedo mounted these steps and tugged open a door. A light, already burning within, sent a bright shaft into the darkness.

Histrina followed him. After the door came a short passage, and then the strangest room she had ever seen. In some ways it was like the priest's confessional room, for there were no windows. The light, though . . . the lamp was a strip, set in the ceiling, and she couldn't see how it worked. Also, since this lamp was already lit, she had imagined there would be people here, but the place was empty. There was a table set against the wall, but on it were not household utensils, but an array of odd-looking shapes, which seemed to be fastened down to it. Other odd-looking objects adorned the walls. There were also some chairs, but Laedo sank down on a low couch large enough to take two.

"Do you live here?" she asked.

He nodded. His head was in his hands.

"How did you come from the other world? Where is the 'ship'?"

He looked up, smiling wearily. "This is the ship. It flies up into the sky where the other worlds are. But it's damaged and won't fly now. I crash-landed here."

She sat down beside him. Her hand seemed to move of its own volition, and began feeling him between his legs through the smooth cloth of the garment he wore. Automatically, absently, he lifted the hem of her gown, slid his hand up and began performing the same service for her.

"Do Ormazd and Ahriman rule in the other worlds, too?"

"Why should they? Not in the way you mean, anyhow . . ."

"Well, *you* belong to the Evil One's horde . . ."

"No, I'm a guest here. The master is intrigued by me. He's helping me."

"Yes, but you belong to Ahriman." She glanced down at their two slowly massaging hands and giggled. "Look what you're doing!"

"What?" He snorted. "There's nothing wicked about it."

"But of *course* it's wicked." She leered at him, and licked her lips. "I like being wicked . . ."

He brushed her off and stood up. "Rubbish!" He seemed annoyed. "It does no one any harm. Doing harm to people is what's wrong."

Histrina leaned back. "Hugger told me the gods don't exist. That it all comes from our own minds. Is that what you think? Perhaps it's right."

Hugger had been no fool, she thought. He was able to think for himself, and not many people could do that. This man Laedo seemed sceptical, too. And he saw no sin in fornication, so . . .

But his next words surprised her. "Your thoughts don't come from within you," he said quietly. "Not entirely. Ormazd and Ahriman *do* exist. They live up in the sky and struggle for domination of Erspia. Here, I'll prove it to you."

He beckoned to her and went through a door in the opposite wall from the one they had come in by. Curiously Histrina followed him up a steep ramp which she found she could climb just as if it had been a staircase, due to the way her sandals clung to its surface. Then they went through a poky little corridor and eventually came out into a large room filled with rows of racks, all laden with variously shaped objects whose purposes she couldn't guess.

Laedo led her to what seemed to be an enormous metal block secured to the floor. He touched a button and part of the block swung open, revealing that it was hollow inside, like a cabinet or kiosk. But its walls, she saw, were more than a foot thick.

"This cabinet is used for storing radioactive materials," he told her. "It's made of a lead compound that stops any kind of radiation known. I was taking it to Harkio, but here on Erspia I've found my own use for it."

She stared at him in incomprehension. "Get inside," he ordered. Then, when she didn't move, he pushed her in, joining her himself and closing the narrow door behind them.

It was dark until he produced from his pocket a strange stick-like gadget which gave off a soft glow and illuminated the interior. They sat on the floor facing one another, knees touching. Laedo gazed absently at her face, as if expecting something.

For what seemed a long time nothing happened, and Histrina was merely bewildered. But then a sense of peace seemed to come over her. The compelling thoughts that for the past hours had been bubbling with gusto in her head—thoughts of lechery, of cruelty, even of murder—died away, and all at once seemed foreign to her.

But the *other* thoughts, those that lately had been defeated and which previously, when supported by the priests, had ruled her—they faded too. Thoughts of good and proper behaviour, of kind actions which she must always seek to do, of social niceties which must always be observed. These, now, seemed just as foreign to her as did the bad thoughts.

She was simply neutral, peaceful and calm.

"Neither Ahriman nor Ormazd can enter here," Laedo said softly.

She delved into her mind. Yes, she *could* summon these thoughts if she wanted to. They were still there. But it took an effort of will. She had to make herself want to savour them. They did not rush in and force themselves on her attention, as formerly they always had.

It was like waking from a dream. Her mind was her own, in a way it never had been before.

"I noticed it very soon after I landed," Laedo said. "Thoughts, urges, pulling and twisting me in two different directions. A lot of people might not have suspected anything, since after all they're the same urges that people are apt to get anyway, with varying degrees of obsession. And of course there's the social thing, which masks it to some extent. The two gods tend to win over social groups, rather than individuals, since people are inevitably influenced by those around them. Paradoxically it's the more individualistic, with naturally stronger minds, who more readily accept impulses from whichever is the enemy god. That's what happened to you, right? You come from a village ruled by Ormazd. But you fell prey to Ahriman."

She nodded, understanding his final words, at least. "So the gods *are* real," she replied wonderingly.

"You could say that. But why is it they can't get into my anti-radiation chamber?" He smiled broadly. "I come in here twice a day just so as to calm down. But for that I'd probably end up like those out there." He jerked a thumb.

She liked the new feeling of calmness, so much so that she was loth for him to open the door. But eventually he did. They stepped out, left the hold and went back to the control cabin-cum-living room. After a few minutes she found desirous thoughts jostling in her again, like a crowd of deranged satyrs.

He carried on talking. "I noticed that Ahriman is stronger during the night and Ormazd during the day. That gave the game away altogether."

He moved to the table and touched one of the queer-looking objects there, spinning a little disk. Histrina gasped as a section of wall suddenly changed colour and then seemed to disappear altogether, so that she was looking beyond it into the starry sky. But surely she should only see another part of this strange house's interior?

"Don't be afraid," Laedo said, noting her amazed expression. "It's only a picture. You're looking at the night zenith."

As he spun the disk again something sprang into being in the centre of the picture and grew swiftly. It became a ball, or globe, with a cylindrical shaft or well projecting from one side of it and pointing almost directly at them.

The object was pale cream in colour and gleamed dully in the starlight, though one side seemed much more brightly lit than the other.

"This is Ahriman," Laedo told her. "Or rather, this is where his thoughts come from. See that cylinder? That's the projector."

Again he flicked switches and spun disks. The picture was replaced by what appeared to be blue sky dotted with fleecy cloud, with the sun flaring fiercely in the centre. The clouds swelled, then vanished and once again there was blackness and stars, with, contradictorily, the sun still glowing, a hard, steady point of light.

And there ahead of them was an identical ball and cylinder, this time shining in the glare of the sun.

"And this is Ormazd," he announced. "The sun is artificial, too. It's no bigger than a medicine ball. That's why shadows are abnormally large here—but of course, that doesn't seem abnormal to you, does it? You probably think the sun circles your world, but in fact all three objects are in a static configuration and Erspia has a twenty-eight hour rotation beneath them. They wouldn't need much power to do that: they are outside the gravity well. Anyway, the configuration seems stable enough. The nearest star is about four light years away."

He uttered the technicalities automatically, careless that she was unable to understand them. She stared at the screen, eyes glazed. "So this is how the gods speak to us," she breathed.

"Twin powers, pulling in opposite directions. Having to pass through the bulk of Erspia attenuates the beams only slightly, just enough so that Ahriman has the advantage by night, and Ormazd by day . . ."

He tailed off. Perhaps she would grasp enough to help her resist. If he could persuade her to make use of the lead cabinet, she might be prevented from falling into the kind of life which was offered here in the encampment.

He still could not fathom what was behind the set-up. It was obviously a contrived travesty of Zoroastrianism, the ancient dualistic religion in which a good god and an evil god fought over possession of the universe. It even used the same names for those gods. That, together with the way their force diminished in alternation with the diurnal rotation of the planetoid, had given him the idea of searching for them beyond the shallow atmosphere.

Earlier he had demonstrated his findings to Hoggora, the man who called himself the High Priest of the Forces of Darkness. Hoggora, to give him his due, possessed an unusually sharp brain. He had quickly understood the notion of spaceships, of viewscreens that could see out into space and even round the curve of the planetoid, and showed by his questions that he understood nearly everything Laedo said to him. He had been delighted at the sight of the Ahrimanic thought-projector, calling it 'Ahriman's mouth'. When Laedo suggested that the evidence was in favour of Ahriman not being a god at all, he had simply shrugged, as though the question didn't interest him.

Laedo had heard of experiments in thought-rays, using low-frequency radiation, but to his knowledge they had never been even moderately successful. The twin beams that bathed this little world were highly sophisticated and fully effective, able to persuade the recipient that the suggestions invading his mind were his own. Laedo did not think the projectors were of human manufacture.

And the inhabitants of Erspia—how had they got here? They all spoke fairly good Argot Galactica, the interstellar language of human intercourse, but had no traditions or legends that told of them arriving from anywhere else. As far as they knew, they had always been on Erspia.

He killed the picture on the screen, replacing it with a view of the camp. By the blazing lights of the fires, banners were raised. Whatever entertainment Hoggora had planned was in progress.

He keyed in sound. A swell of screams and triumphant, hoarse shouts filled the cabin. It was the same every night. There were always plenty of prisoners to satisfy the horde's bloodlust.

Laedo wondered what it would be like to give way entirely to sensuousness, greed and violence.

He blanked out the screen and turned to Histrina. "Okay," he said with a sigh, "let's get to bed."

In the following days Laedo suffered a number of disappointments. Histrina consented, at first, to join him in his twice-daily sessions in the lead cabinet—including one at midnight, to ward off Ahriman at his strongest. But after a while he sensed her reluctance to continue. Once she disappeared into the encampment for an entire day, to return at dawn, flushed, bright-eyed and exhilarated.

He did not ask her what she had been doing. He had come to realize that a person's eventual allegiance to one god or the other owed something to an inner disposition as well as to social influences. The Ormazdian priests had become adept at blocking sinful thoughts, and likewise the worshippers of Ahriman had learned to block any good or worthy thoughts.

Something in Histrina liked Ahriman better than it liked Ormazd.

His second disappointment concerned the work Hoggora had ordered an artisan to do for him. Laedo's forced stay on Erspia had lasted several weeks now. When his star engine failed he had at first suspected something amiss with the fuel rods, which he had bought cheap from a roadside vendor. But he had checked them out and found them all right.

There had been nothing for it but to strip down the engine. He had cursed himself mightily for not providing himself with a proper tool kit, but fortunately the fault had come to light as soon as he got the cowling off. A transductor had fractured. It was lucky the spilled energy had not melted down the entire ship.

It would be no good trying to weld it. Essentially, however, the part was simple—merely a rectangular conduit about six feet long, with a precisely aligned arrangement of internal flanges. There were a number of skilled metal workers in the camp, and Laedo hoped that mild steel, if he put a refrigeration jacket on it, would hold out long enough to get him to the nearest inhabited star, where he could get one made of the proper HCferric.

The artisan bungled the job. The flanges were much too rough, and were not precisely positioned. The energy hazing from the fuel rods, instead of being whirled into a plasmic vortex, would instead erode the pipe before he got half a light year.

He debated whether to inform Hoggora of the metal worker's failure. Hoggora would likely have the fellow burned alive for it. Laedo was not sure what his own fate would be, either. Hoggora regarded him as a pet, an exotic plaything. He was entranced by Laedo's tales of other worlds among the stars and plainly meant to visit them himself when the ship was in order—as well, possibly, as make a pilgrimage to Ahriman's mouth, where he felt sure he would be well received as High Priest.

One afternoon, four days after he had accepted Histrina into his household, Laedo came out of the anti-radiation cabinet and trudged to the main cabin, where he found her just emerging from her bed. He took some coffee and food slabs from the dispenser, gave them to her and took some for himself, munching the slabs absently while he gazed at the viewscreen, which was focused on the encampment.

There was a great deal of activity in the camp. Hoggora was planning one of his periodic crusades in which he would mark off some section of Erspia and attempt to destroy all vestige of Ormazdian worship inside it. A constant war was being waged on the planetoid, perpetually inconclusive because the Ahrimanics, for all their ferocity, were matched by a stout defence on the part of the Ormazdian villages—who in turn would, if they could, annihilate the servants of the Evil One.

Histrina slurped the coffee, enjoying its novel flavour (the only beverage on Erspia was a weak beer brewed from maize, the staple crop). Laedo's mind was on the orbiting thought projectors. It occurred to him that he might find what he needed there. Tools, materials, repair robots, most likely. The projectors had been there a long time and there would have to be some provision for maintenance.

His ship, even though it couldn't go into star drive, could certainly travel a few hundred miles on its manoeuvring engine, even a few thousand miles. It was worth trying, especially since the only alternative was to stay here until he could get a serviceable transductor made, which might be never.

Energised by this thought, he sprang up and made his way to the engine compartment, where he levered in place the baffles that would prevent the fuel rods from delivering any of their power through the cracked transductor. They would now service only the close manoeuvring engine.

He spent some time checking the pipes and joints. Quite a bit of energy haze had leaked into the works generally. It wouldn't do to get total failure a hundred miles or so up.

What of Histrina? Might as well bring her along with him, he thought. If he got what he wanted he'd take her on to Harkio, rescuing her from this damned planetoid, though he didn't know why he should bother.

Otherwise, they were back to square one.

By the time he had finished, Erspia's terminator line was approaching and the point-source sun was about to slip below the horizon. Histrina, when he returned to the cabin, was lounging on a couch, staring vacantly. On seeing him she smiled and invitingly opened her legs.

Laedo ignored the gesture. He moved to the control board, unlocked it, and keyed in the power. A fuzzy, high-pitched note sounded beyond the wall.

"What's that?" Histrina asked, sitting up suddenly.

He pointed to the screen. "Watch."

She clung to the couch as the view on the screen swung, dipped, then fell away. The ground vanished.

"What is it?" she screeched.

"We're flying. Didn't I tell you this ship could go to the stars?"

"You said it didn't work any more."

"Not to get to the stars. We're going somewhere nearer."

Unlike a normal planet's, Erspia's shadow cast an expanding, not narrowing, cone into space, as a consequence of the sun's tiny size. Laedo had decided to make for the Ahrimanic projector rather than the Ormazdian one, so as to avoid approaching that sun, which at close range might well be dangerous. The manoeuvring engine strained as it lifted the ship up the gravity well. Laedo became afraid that the small motor might not make it, but then the gravity field suddenly ended, cut off sharp in the manner typical of gravity generators. From now on there was only the natural attraction of the planetoid to contend with, and the ship accelerated easily.

He located the small disk of the projector, locked a course on it, then turned back to Histrina. She was still clutching the couch and staring at the screen, which now showed only stars, the sun having disappeared.

"It will only take a few minutes," he told her.

"Where are we going?"

"Hoggora calls it Ahriman's mouth."

"Ohhh . . ." Her eyes opened wide in surprise.

He returned to the board, curious to see the object at close quarters. As it swelled, he became aware of a malevolent bubbling in his mind, like a spring of evil water breaking through from below. Conscious of Histrina at his back; he suddenly experienced thoughts concerning her that were so violent and disgusting that they shocked the more detached part of him.

He fought to push the feelings away—he had became adept at turning aside Ahrimanic suggestions. But the impulse grew stronger, became a gloating, rejoicing sense of wickedness which threatened to overwhelm him.

Of course! he thought. *I imagined Ahriman was stronger by night because Erspia's bulk absorbs the beam as it passed through. Instead it's because one is nearer to Ahriman at night. The beam has to emanate in a cone if it's to cover the whole planetoid. It's more concentrated towards the apex!*

A stinging blow in the back of his neck made him stagger. He spun round. Histrina was crouched, her face twisted in a grimace, a knife from the dining table in her hand. She had stabbed him in the neck with it.

Luckily it was not a very sharp piece of cutlery, neither had she used it very expertly. Feeling the blood trickle down his back, Laedo was momentarily seized with thoughts of what he would do to Histrina. He lunged, trapped her wrist, then twisted her hand till she dropped the knife. He put his hands round her neck and began to squeeze.

Oh, he was enjoying it! He squeezed harder, till her tongue edged out between her teeth. Then, with a supreme effort, he let her go and stepped back.

She collapsed, coughing painfully and holding her throat. But it didn't take her long to get to her feet again. She threw herself at him, her fingers hooked into claws, the nails seeking to gouge out his eyes. Laedo threshed with his arms, fending her off while tussling with the maddening impulses that were growing stronger by the second.

The thought projector was looming large. On the screen Laedo could see that the spherical surface was ribbed and striated. He attempted to get to the controls, but by now Histrina, howling in an ululating note of savagery, was on her knees, trying to mangle his testicles with both hands. He kicked her hard in the stomach.

She rolled over, retching. For some moments Laedo was torn between what he wanted to do and what he knew he must do. What he wanted to do was to get hold of Histrina and subject her to the worst experiences a totally depraved mind could devise. In the end, he did what he knew he should do. He moved a control wheel, and the ship swung aside.

Out of the path of the beam.

He sank to the floor, holding his head in his hands. Nausea overwhelmed him. It was as though a spring of evil-smelling liquid, that had soaked his feelings and driven him crazy, was draining back to where it had come from, into his censored unconscious, no longer prodded and awakened by Ahriman's lance.

Histrina did not calm down quite so quickly. When her pain abated she continued to make animal-like gestures, clawing the air with her hands as though to strike at him, and hissing like a snake. But after a few minutes her gestures became mechanical and empty, then ceased altogether.

"Do you feel any better?" Laedo asked.

She nodded.

"We were too close to Ahriman," he explained, noting as he spoke that her eyes still gleamed in a rather unpleasant way. "He was too strong for us. Ormazd's influence is so weak out here."

He adjusted the screen. The Ahrimanic sphere appeared in side view, the chute-like shaft projecting from it like the barrel of a gun.

He wondered what flying up the Ormazdian beam would be like. Paroxysms of benevolence, perhaps.

Carefully he scrutinized the sphere for some sign of an entrance, and spotted a circular crack that was, possibly, a hatch. If it would open he could presumably get inside without exposing himself to thought projection again. But he realized that his action in coming here had lacked discrimination, had been too subjective. He was now frightened of what he might find inside the Ahrimanic stronghold.

The sphere of Ormazd sounded safer.

He turned the ship away and set a course for the opposite side of Erspia. As they passed out of shadow the sun became visible, glaring against the stars.

"Don't worry, we'll be all right," he told her without conviction. "We're going to Ormazd instead."

"Why are you doing this?"

As succinctly as was practicable, Laedo explained that he was seeking help to escape from Erspia and return to the world he had come from. "Or rather, worlds," he ended. "There are hundreds of inhabited ones out there, all of them a hundred times bigger than the one you know. You'll like it, Histrina. Erspia is like never leaving your own back yard. It's amazing you've turned out as bright as you are."

He could see the idea appealed to her.

The sun grew near, and the viewscreen automatically tuned down its increasing brilliance. Laedo took care to stay clear of the thought cone, and soon found himself facing a ribbed, striated globe that was, to appearances, identical to the one he had just left.

He pondered on how to gain entrance. There was a ploy for such situations which often worked on human space vehicles, but there was no clue as to whether this one was of human or alien manufacture.

The ploy was to hurl a mass of radio signals at the lock, if there was one, which would often respond by opening. Laedo had a recording of the most likely signals (such items could be purchased at any space port for a paltry sum) and he fed it into his transmitter.

Hopefully he edged his ship closer to the hatch. The sphere itself was large; several times the size of his own ship, and larger, in fact, than a decent-sized cargo vessel. Large enough, he reminded himself, to be manned.

At first nothing happened. Then the hatch began to rotate. Instead of withdrawing or projecting, however, it seemed to roll aside, leaving a gaping pit.

"Karaka!" Laedo cried.

Histrina frowned. "What?"

"We hit the spot." Laedo had been quoting from a numbers game. He put out landing legs so the ship could grip the wall of the sphere, then put down. He found he didn't need to use sticky-extrusion: the sphere was magnetically permeable and the legs were able to clamp on it that way.

Opening a locker, he took out a suit and a weapon. "You stay here," he told Histrina. "I'm going to take a look."

"No! Don't leave me on my own!"

He held up the suit. "There's no air out there. You have to wear one of these to breathe. You'll be scared."

"No, I won't."

He sighed, took out a spare suit and threw it to her. "Get into it, then."

Fastening up the slim suit for her, and connecting her to him by a line in case she lost her footing and went floating off into space, he led her through the passageway airlock. They stepped down onto the metal surface of the sphere.

Histrina was not reassured by the lifeline. She floundered, and then panicked on seeing herself surrounded by such a strange and alien environment. Laedo took her arm and guided her to the entrance, showing her how to place her feet so that she wouldn't cast herself adrift.

He had to manhandle her over the lip of the circular pit that led to the inside of the sphere. Once standing on its inner wall, however, normal weight returned. As he had expected, there was a manipulated gravity field inside.

The tunnel was perhaps ten yards long, and it was lighted by a pale green glow. When they had reached the halfway mark Laedo felt a puffing on his body that told him the passage was filling with air, or at least some kind of gas. Glancing behind him, he saw that the lid had rolled back in place. He bit his lip. This he hadn't expected. it looked as though they might be trapped.

He needn't have worried. When they had almost reached the end of the tunnel a similar lid there rolled aside. Beyond it was a level, well-lighted area. And blocking the way, standing in a line to confront him and Histrina, were four men. The cast of their features was similar to that of the natives of Erspia, except that they were somewhat paler, and their hair was cropped short. They wore long white gowns, cinched at the waist, and on the chest of each of these simple garments was a golden sun blaze.

One of the men held out his hands, palms upward. Hesitantly, he spoke.

"Do you come . . . from the Great One?"

Inside his helmet, Laedo smiled. it was tempting to give the answer the man clearly expected, but he knew he would never be able to sustain the deception, and he shook his head.

A wave of reassurance swept over him. He knew he had nothing to fear from these people.

It was also a great relief to find that the keepers of the projector were, after all, human.

"I can well understand that the mental environment on Erspia was strange to you," Kwenis said mildly, pouring a fragrant, hot liquid into little cups from a tall, elegant pot. "Bewildering, even. I am taking your story at face value, of course."

Laedo sat in a tidily furnished room. Kwenis passed one of the cups across the low table between them. The beverage, almost purple in colour, was less bitter than coffee but refreshing. It was some species of tea, Laedo concluded.

He had been in the projector station for nearly an hour. Kwenis had taken him on a tour of the place, showing him the massive thought projector, the living quarters, and an installation which Laedo was certain was a star drive. There seemed to be a staff of eight on the station, four of them women with whom Histrina at this moment was also taking tea.

Kwenis called himself Chief Guardian of Ormazd. The other staff members were also guardians of Ormazd, apparently.

It was clear to Laedo that Kwenis was also vastly relieved that he was not, after all, receiving a visit from the 'Great One', whoever that might be.

"But what's it all *for?*" he asked. "Who's behind it? The 'Great One', I suppose. Who's he?"

Kwenis sipped his tea reflectively. "I will tell you the whole story. 'Great One' is a reverential term for a being whom otherwise we know as 'Klystar'. Klystar is a naturally evolved creature, like ourselves, but one with superior intelligence, so we believe, or at any rate superior ability. Klystar leads a roaming existence. Some time ago he happened to visit this region of the galaxy, and during his stay here he became interested in certain facets of human psychology. In particular, he was intrigued by the human mind's suggestibility to thoughts, no matter where those thoughts come from. To Klystar it was most curious, for instance, that one person can persuade another of something, irrespective of whether or not it is reasonable. Most beings, in Klystar's experience, form their thoughts and conduct independently of any swaying influence, as he himself does. We are queer creatures indeed from Klystar's point of view. At any rate, he set up an experiment to investigate this phenomenon. He fashioned Erspia, and put people upon it. Above the planetoid he poised the two great thought projectors, one beaming what in conventional morality are 'good' thoughts, the other 'bad' thoughts. And he named them after the good and bad gods of a dualist human religion from a time when this morality was the rule in human society.

"But Klystar decided to leave before the experiment reached its final stage. So he placed us in the projector housings to act as servitors, to maintain the projectors should they malfunction, to carry out the final stage of the experiment, and to record its results. If, after a certain time, he had not returned, we were free to leave, and for that purpose he also gave us a star drive, as he did the guardians of Ahriman."

"And what is the final stage?"

"The final stage is to switch off the projectors, and then to monitor events below to see whether the attitudes and beliefs they have inculcated will persist."

Laedo was fascinated. "So all those people down there are just experimental animals!" He shook his head, smiling sardonically. "And when are the projectors due to be switched off?"

Kwenis looked uncomfortable. "According to schedule, thirty years ago. But we have not done it."

"Indeed? Why not?"

Placing down his cup, Kwenis fidgeted, and then sighed. "As a guardian of Ormazd, I am unable to lie. We would have obeyed Klystar's instructions and switched off our projector, no matter what it cost us. But the Ahrimanic servitors were of a different mind and refused to do so. We are fearful of what the consequences would be down below if *only* the Ahrimanic mode of thought were to operate—though, as a matter of fact, switching one or other of the projectors on again for a short period was to have constituted an additional sub-programme. So we have left matters as they are. To be honest, it is in our interest to do so."

"Oh? How is that?"

Kwenis raised his eyebrows. "Why, because we are immortal for as long as the experiment remains in force. How else could Klystar ensure that we can service his equipment for centuries? When the experiment is finished, the life-giving force is withdrawn also."

After absorbing this, Laedo snorted. "Perhaps motivation is another aspect of human behaviour that Klystar didn't understand," he suggested acidly.

Kwenis shrugged. "Perhaps. As I said, we would have obeyed. The backwash from the projector irradiates us, you know, and makes us truthful, honest and conscientious. But with the Ahrimanic servitors it is another matter, and there I can well believe that Klystar miscalculated. It is lucky you did not fall into their hands, for one can imagine how it is with them, steeped in deceit, selfishness and hatred. It is a wonder they have not all killed one another, but we know they are still alive, for every year they send us the obligatory signal. Klystar, no doubt, saw to their survival. As for ourselves, what harm is done? It is plain that Klystar is not going to return. We are happy here, living in harmony with one another, in benevolence, truthfulness and chastity. And our lives do not end."

"The losers, of course, are the people on Erspia, who don't have possession of their own minds."

"Neither do we," Kwenis reminded him. "Does anyone? That was the point of Klystar's experiment. And anyway, it is better for them than if Ahriman were to reign supreme. That is the alternative."

Nodding, Laedo decided to drop the subject. It was not politic to criticise the people he was hoping would help him.

"My own star drive is broken," he said, coming straight to the point. "Can you help me repair it? It's a simple sort of repair. Then I can be away from here—I'm sure you don't want me as a permanent guest."

"I shall have to see. Lylos, Dugas and Markeer are our technical experts. I'll ask them what they can do. Meantime I'll show you to the sleeping quarters you can occupy while here."

He rose, then turned to Laedo, blushing slightly. "You will, of course, occupy separate sleeping quarters from your companion's. I know you have been down on Erspia where licentiousness is rife, but we can brook no such behaviour here!"

"What?" Laedo rose too, a disbelieving grin on his face. "But you just admitted Ormazdian morality is all arbitrary—the product of a machine!"

Shaking his head, Kwenis put up his hand as though thrusting away such an interpretation. "We are chaste, and kind to one another. We take seriously our role as Guardians of Ormazd."

Oh boy, Laedo thought, wouldn't Klystar like to see this! Knowledge conquered by suggestion! But he said no more, and obediently allowed Kwenis to lead him away.

The next 'day', as the guardians reckoned time, was as frustrating to Laedo as had been his experience with the metal-worker on Erspia. The 'technicians' prided themselves on being able to repair the projector and any of the equipment on the station. But their repair work, he discovered, consisted of pulling out malfunctioning modules and plugging in replacements from a ready-made stock, an operation which was required on average once every ten years. Klystar, like many technically proficient beings, did not have a fetish about sophistication. The whole thing could have been handled automatically with a little built-in redundancy, or, with better components, could have been made unnecessary. From the look of the station, Laedo guessed it had been put together in a cursory, even careless, manner. Hence the human crew: they were good enough, so why take more trouble?

When Laedo showed them his broken transductor, they clucked, tutted, and shook their heads.

He told Histrina. She became depressed. Already she had promised herself a wider world than Erspia. He detected, in her disappointment, a private fury.

"So when do we go back to Erspia?" she asked bitterly.

"We don't go back," he said in a low voice.

"How. . . ?"

"There's still a star drive here. I can hope to persuade the guardians to use it."

"Or we can steal it," she said quickly.

"I don't see how."

"No . . . you wouldn't."

Her tone was contemptuous. She walked away, her bare feet leaving damp imprints on the shiny floor.

Two days later Laedo's proposal to the guardians that they should abandon their long vigil clearly was not going to get anywhere. Further, it became apparent that since his own drive could not be repaired, the guardians expected him and Histrina to return to Erspia before too long.

That night, he fell asleep mulling things over. Later, he was awakened by a hand shaking his shoulder.

Histrina stood there. She swayed slightly. Her face had a glassy look. In her right hand was his gun.

"It's done," she said.

He sat up. "What are you doing with my gun?" he demanded harshly. She must have taken it from the locker where their spacesuits were kept, he realized. She turned away, and beckoned.

Silently he followed her. She took him to the sleeping cubicle adjoining his. On the pallet, covered by a thin sheet, lay Lylos, one of the guardians who had been introduced to him as a technician.

Histrina pointed to his head. Laedo leaned closer.

Blood trickled from a neat hole bored just to the rear of Lylos' temple. It was a close-focus shot from Laedo's handgun.

Laedo had seen violent death many times on Erspia. He tried not to be shocked, especially when he thought of the pitiless experiment on which the guardians were engaged. But despite himself he *was* shocked. More than that, he felt frightened at having Histrina by his side, still holding the gun.

Wordlessly she led him to the other cubicles, first the men's, then the women's. In each skull the same neat hole had been drilled. Histrina had brought the centuried life of the entire projector station staff to an end.

"Now we can leave," she said calmly.

He stared at her. "How could you do it?" he said blankly. "Especially in here . . . where Ormazd reigns. Didn't you feel his influence?"

"He doesn't reign over *me*." Her face lost its look of trance. Her eyes flashed, became alive. "Ormazd can't touch me now. Something happened to me when we flew towards Ahriman. He got deep inside me."

Laedo said nothing. Perhaps it could happen, he thought. At such intensity the beam might work a permanent change in someone—if they were receptive to it.

He was becoming more impressed with Histrina's mental

sharpness. It was remarkable enough that she had guessed the gun to be a weapon, when there were only lances, swords and bows and arrows on Erspia. But that she had learned to use it so quickly . . .

This question was answered when she took him into her own sleeping cubicle. The walls were sprayed and splashed with molten material where she had experimented with the gun's focusing ring.

"Here's where I practised," she told him. "Simple, really, isn't it?"

He held out his hand. "Give it to me, Histrina."

She drew the gun back, holding it behind her. "Oh, no, I want to keep it. Give it to me as a present."

Laedo sighed. Histrina had become clever and evil. He was going to have to learn not to turn his back to her.

The first job was to get rid of the bodies. This they did together by the simple expedient of throwing them out of the hatch towards Erspia. They would, with fair probability, end up falling through the shallow atmosphere to land as flaming meteors.

Laedo realized that he had acquired a valuable property in the station. Thought projection was a technique with limitless possibilities, once it was understood. There were people who would pay him a vast sum for the projector. He set himself to studying the station's controls. They were, he found, surprisingly simple to operate. Klystar had modelled them on the human technology then currently available—for the benefit of the human crew, no doubt—which wasn't so very different from today's. Laedo didn't bother himself over where Klystar had obtained the human beings to people his exercise in practical psychology, but the drive unit, too, appeared similar to that he was used to.

Not wanting to lose his own ship, he employed a trick familiar to spacemen, manoeuvring it round the globe to reposition it precisely on the axis of thrust, directly opposite the drive unit. In any other position it would have been torn away once the globe was in motion, for the drive unit's energy field would only partially engulf it. If he had aligned it correctly it would now stay put, carried along by the globe's velocity.

Within hours he was ready to take off. Histrina still had the gun, but she seemed well disposed towards him and he didn't feel too uneasy—and anyway she needed him, he told himself. He abandoned thoughts of luring her back down to Erspia and leaving her there. She was too sharp for that. But he would try to buy some psychological rehabilitation for her in Harkio, he decided.

One thing he left till last. He had found himself reluctant to switch off the projector, knowing the field would be left to purely Ahrimanic influences. But what else could he do?

So, at the last minute, when he sat before the station's control board ready to energise the engine, the projector was still emitting. But already he had taken a key which he had found hanging from the neck of the dead Kwenis, and had opened the lid of a sturdy box bolted to the board. Inside the box was a massive switch of the old-fashioned lever type.

Laedo's arm seemed extraordinarily heavy as he moved his hand to the switch. The lever seemed to resist him, and he thought for a moment that it might be corroded in place. Then, with a clunk, it shifted.

The invisible mental searchlight went out. Without pause he energised. The globe of Ormazd shot away from Erspia, into the interstellar realm and towards Harkio.

The sun had set and Hoggora, High Priest of the Forces of Darkness, felt vigorous and confident. True, the villagers, contrary to Drosh's report, had assembled a force to match his own. He was faced, in fact, by an alliance of villages, and this would be a battle to go down in legend. But darkness had come, and the darkness always made him feel strong. He looked forward with joy to the carnage that was about to commence.

His cavalry was lined up on one side of a shallow river, the infantry jostling behind. On the other side of the water was a less colourful, but more rigidly disciplined parade. It was a case of ferocity versus fortitude, as it had always been. But this time the outcome would give one side or the other a decided advantage for years to come.

Beyond the silent ranks, the priests of Ormazd, in their tall, coiffed headdresses, raised their faces to heaven in rapt prayer. Hoggora prayed, too, hurling his voice hoarsely to that point in space where he knew the Mouth of Ahriman hovered.

"Ahriman! Aid us!"

And then, as if in answer to his supplication, an event took place that caused the entire assembly, on both sides, to pause and become stock-still. It was an invisible event, but one that was yet felt by everyone present. In the perpetual tussle that took place in each man's mind, one of the contending factors abruptly went missing. Ahriman alone remained, to exult in his victory.

It was as if a shadow of evil swept over the world, a shadow that could never be lifted. The priests, sensing the death of the Good God, wailed in disbelieving horror. The ranks arrayed before them shivered and moaned as they, too, felt the strength of their lord leave them.

But among Hoggora's army an incredible chafing joy took hold. Hoggora screamed a command, howling in triumph. A volley of arrows whistled across the river. Lances were levelled, pennants flew. With a great shout, the Horde of the Evil One surged across the shallow water to claim its own.

TWO

Orchid Paradise

The drive had been in operation for only minutes when a mechanism behind the panel of the control board chattered and a sheet of parchment-like material came stuttering out of a slot.

Laedo snatched it up as it floated floorwards. Words, still smoking, had been etched or burned into the sheet in argot galactica.

Experiment incomplete, they read. *Return station to duty.*

Laedo stared. It had not occurred to him that the projector station might be able to monitor the performance of its staff.

How to reply? Laedo searched the panel. The mechanism had not spoken out loud, so he presumed there would be a writing plate or something even more primitive, such as a keyboard. But he found nothing. Finally, in exasperation, he responded as if to a normal control device.

"The experiment has been abandoned. The staff are all dead," he said, raising his voice.

After a pause there came more chattering and another sheet of parchment was extruded.

Must report to Klystar, he read. Then he felt movement under his feet.

The dials on the board were shifting their settings. With a yell he seized control levers and tried to correct the course, but it was no good. The station was changing direction and all the flight parameters—velocity flow, fuel rate, flight tensor—were being adjusted by an unseen, expert power.

Not back to Erspia. Not towards Harkio. To where?

He groaned and sank back in the pilot's seat.

The door slid open. Histrina stepped into the room, her gun thrust into the belt of her gauzy shift-like gown, dimpling her soft belly.

"What's wrong?" she asked, in the cool and self-possessed voice she had acquired since the killings.

"I don't know where the hell we're going—if anywhere."

"I thought we were going to your home world. To Harkio."

"So did I. But this thing has a mind of its own. I think it's trying to take us to Klystar, the being who made Erspia. Only I don't suppose it even knows where Klystar is."

"Well, *do* something," Histrina said, in a tone whose sharpness surprised and even frightened him a little.

Raising his face, and ignoring Histrina's puzzlement at seeing him address thin air, he spoke again.

"Klystar went away a long time ego. There's no one to report to. Hand back control of the station to me."

This time there was no chattering of words being burned onto parchment, and no change in the dial readings. "It's no good," Laedo muttered.

Histrina clenched her fists in frustration. "Think of something *else*," she insisted bitingly.

"I'll have to see if I can get the casing off and jigger about with the cybernetics somehow. The trouble is, putting it out of action might disconnect the drive unit controls as well. We'd be stranded."

"Look!" said Histrina.

Over the control panel a part of wall had changed colour from grey to smudgy white, forming a wide oval patch. The oval cleared and became glasslike. It was a viewscreen.

In it, Laedo saw what he presumed lay ahead of them: black space dotted with stars. Then, to the accompaniment of more movement under their feet, the view swivelled round.

Suddenly they were looking at a planet, shining in the darkness, lit on one side by an unseen sun.

"It's *Erspia!*" Histrina cried. "We're back at Erspia!"

"No, we couldn't be." Laedo inspected the dials with a frown. "We haven't gone back, not unless these readings are all wrong. We're thousands of miles away."

For all that, it *did* look a lot like Erspia. Now he spotted where the planet's daytime illumination came from: a point source of light, orbiting the globe not far away. It was the Erspia system in duplicate, and automatically he began to see it not as a planet proper but as a spherically shaped planetoid, even though the screen gave no ranging figures from which to estimate size.

"Erspia looks brownish-green from space," he said to Histrina. "Look close at that planet. It's mottled in different colours."

"I don't see."

Laedo wasn't sure if he saw the colours either now. Perhaps it had been an optical effect, a sort of shading of phantom hues. But the globe was definitely lighter in tone than Erspia. It was almost pastel.

"It's obvious Klystar made more than one world," he said tonelessly. "We'll wait till the station parks itself in orbit or whatever. Then I'll have a go at the casing."

But the station didn't go into orbit. Laedo gave a hiss of indrawn breath as the planetoid's globe shape swooped nearer.

They were going in—fast!

"Look out!" he yelled to the hidden controller. "There's a planet ahead! We're going to crash!"

"What's happening?" Histrina shrieked.

"We're out of control. Quick—get into this chair." He pointed to the padded, braced seat next to his. It wasn't much protection, but it was better than standing.

Histrina disregarded his advice. "I'll fix that thing," she snarled. She pulled the gun from her waistband and pointed it at the control board as the worldlet swelled and swelled on the screen, blotting out the ebony margin that had surrounded it.

"No!" Laedo jumped up and began wrestling with her, forcing the nozzle of the gun away from the control board. "That won't help! Stop it!"

Again he felt the floor shift beneath his feet, then a slight pressure. He knew that these indications were leaks through the artificial gravity from much more powerful acceleration forces that would have crushed them both instantly. Either the station was changing course, or it was decelerating.

"It's all right!" he shouted. "Put the gun away, Histrina!"

Dubiously she obeyed. The sunlit side of the planetoid was now so close that blurry surface features could be made out— fuzzy mottled colours, lavender, light green, daffodil yellow, swaying and sliding past. Then, abruptly, it all streaked aside and they were once more looking into space, with the point-source sun glaring out at them.

The station had turned itself over. It was coming down for a landing, right side up.

Laedo seated himself back at the control board. Experimentally he worked a set of slides whose use he had been unable to discover before. As he now guessed, they controlled the viewscreen. In moments he learned how to direct the scope downwards, so that he was able once more to survey the surface.

This definitely was *not* Erspia. The projector station was descending gently, with a lateral drift so that it appeared to skim over a landscape now clearly visible in all its features. It was a world of flamboyant jungle—though not a jungle of trees, but instead of what appeared to be gigantic blooms or orchids, riotous with colour. At first Laedo thought he had got the focus wrong and was scanning a tropical garden from an apparent height of a foot or two, but no, the viewpoint was their true one, hundreds or thousands of feet in the air. Interspersing the growths were clear patches carpeted with pale green grass or moss, and here and there, azure lakes.

He felt Histrina lean over him. "Isn't it lovely?" she murmured. Her arm hung limply, the gun still clasped in her fingers.

Laedo wondered if the projector station could survive a planetary landing in Earth-normal gravity. Presumably it was built for space, without much by way of internal bracing. Still, it *was* of sturdy construction otherwise . . .

Histrina was cooing and mooing as if at a fireworks display. They had begun to dip into the forest, brushing through the huge, fleshy orchids, tearing through titanic petals, ripping through tangles of sunlit vines, becoming engulfed in colour. There was a sudden jar as the station struck the ground. On the screen was nothing but a flurry. Something had gone wrong; they were tumbling over and over, rolling through the jungle, snapping and breaking the apparently unresisting growths— even though the artificial gravity within the control room kept Laedo and Histrina sitting and standing calmly, undisturbed by the violent motions.

Fascinated, they watched as the tumbling spectacle slowed and became still. They had come to a stop.

Once at rest, the scope showed an expanse of close-cropped, light green grass among which were patches of moss. Laedo worked the cursors again. The spherical station had settled on its side—if the location of the drive unit could be taken to represent its underneath—in a large clearing. Wide mossy trails seemed to wander into the jungle. There was a glimpse of blue water.

And that jungle . . .

Actually it was not, as he had first thought, close-packed. One could have strolled through it with ease. The place was like some alien Eden, a flower forest whose trees were giant blooms, whose huge orchids replaced timber boles and trunks.

And the colours! Nowhere did they clash, nowhere were they even glaring, but the total effect was breathtaking. Pale colours, yellows, ochres, cyan, lavender, sometimes glowingly transparent, shot through with stronger tones—scarlet, saffron, mazarine. For long minutes Laedo and Histrina gazed entranced, while Laedo slowly panned the cursor.

"Come on," Histrina said eagerly. "Let's go outside!"

"We'll have to check the atmosphere first."

"We'll have to do what?" Mystified, Histrina stared at him.

He sighed. "I suppose it's bound to be all right, on second thought. This is one of Klystar's productions, after all."

"I've never seen this part of Erspia before."

"This *isn't* Erspia, Histrina," Laedo said wearily. "I just tried to explain. It's another world, something like Erspia, only different. Do you understand that?"

"I suppose so." She frowned, then brightened. "I wonder if there are people here?"

"So do I."

Getting out was easier than he had thought it would be. They walked the corridor to the hatch which was the only portal Laedo had found in the whole station so far. He opened it and poked his head out.

The sensation was peculiar. The hatch was about thirty feet off the ground, but it was on the under-curve of the station, facing downwards. The artificial gravity kept him standing on the floor of the corridor, but this was upside down to the ground, at an angle of about forty-five degrees, so that the landscape appeared to rear crazily over him. Once his head cleared the skin of the station, however, the planetoid's gravity took over and his head and his body were tugged in different directions.

He was pondering the problem of how to reach the ground when Histrina casually solved it for him. "What do you think this is for?" she said, and pulled a lever behind him. Something rattled out from a slot below the hatch. It was a folding stairway which flapped, swayed and dropped, until it offered a steep but negotiable route to the floor of the clearing, complete with handrail.

He stepped down carefully, holding on to the rail. He could feel Histrina's tread behind him, urging him on.

On the ground they stopped to take in their surroundings. The air was delightful: light, invigorating, filled with delicate scents. Laedo saw that the glimpse of blue he had seen was a lake in a meadow or parkland, partly hidden by a fringe of the giant orchids. Only in that direction did the close horizon betray the small size of this world. Elsewhere, because of the way the jungle hid everything, they could have been on a full-sized planet.

Laedo looked up at the projector station, backing away to take it in. Evidently it was perfectly capable of coping with the stresses of normal gravity, though whether this was due to structural strength or help from the internal gravity field he did not know. It reared over the tops of the titanic flowers; but somehow, now that it was down on the ground, it seemed less bulky than it had in space. It was, in fact, about the size of a small passenger liner, or perhaps an interworld shuttle.

Large enough, he supposed, to be a miniature world in itself for the eight people who had staffed it.

It seemed to have suffered no harm from rolling through the jungle. His own ship, though, was missing. It had been torn off. No doubt it lay in the jungle somewhere.

Given time, he might be able to gain control over the station's drive unit. At least he'd better be able to do it, he told himself fiercely. Otherwise he'd be stuck here for good.

He turned back to look at the jungle again. Only now did the silence of the place strike him. There was no singing of birds, such as had been ever-present on Erspia. There was no buzzing of insects. In fact, no sign of animal life at all.

That air, though . . . breathing in deeply, he felt his senses tingle. It was like wine, it was like . . . where had he breathed air such as that before? He could only think of one of the pleasure houses back in civilisation, its air loaded with molecules to stimulate the appetite for food, sex or whatever.

Evidently Histrina was enjoying it, too. She gave a happy sigh. Then she sauntered towards the nearby orchids.

But suddenly she stopped, and stared like a stalking cat. "Look!" she hissed.

Laedo followed her gaze and caught up with her. Two figures had entered the jungle from the direction of the park-like grassland. They were tall, fair-haired and fair-skinned, though tanned by the sun. Silently, with graceful, light steps, they walked between the monstrous growths like fairies in a paradisical garden.

One was a man, one a woman. Both were completely naked, a circumstance which caused Histrina to giggle lickerishly. "Look at him," she whispered aside to Laedo. "He's stiff!"

And so he was. Laedo stared at his feet, aware that the was probably about to witness an act the couple would regard as private. But what happened next removed his sense of reserve.

The two had reached the mouth of a fleshy orchid, a glowing pale lavender in colour. Reminding Laedo once more of fairies, they proceeded to climb through its thick petals and into the roomy bell, vanishing from view.

The huge flower trembled. From within came cries which Laedo would have interpreted as cries of agony and despair, had he not known better.

Histrina turned to him, her faced flushed, her eyes glistening. "Come on!" she urged, as she grabbed him by the wrist and tugged him at a half run towards the jungle.

She selected the first orchid they came to, an almost globular flower of a translucent, luminous yellow. She had to reach up to its entrance, which was a narrow gap or porticoed slot, and it yielded reluctantly to her arms like the jaws of a snapdragon, as she hauled herself up and in, her legs kicking as she wriggled her way inside.

Moments later her head and shoulders reappeared, thrusting through the portico lips. Apparently she had discarded her gown. Her hair, face, and shoulders were dusted with a fine yellow powder. It was, Laedo realized, pollen.

"Come on in, quick!" she shouted, in a note of almost hysterical urgency.

Unsure of what was happening, Laedo hesitated. But Histrina would brook no delay. She bared her teeth in a grimace. At the same time, her arm poked through the entrance. She was holding the gun, and it pointed right at him.

"Come on in here, I say!" she screeched.

It was with something of a shock that Laedo recognised the expression on Histrina's face. She was transfigured with lust. Naked, raging lust, as compelling as an animal's fear, sweeping away all logic.

Now, he reasoned, might not be the time to cross Histrina. Besides, something was working on him, too. As they approached the orchid he had become aware of its aroma, a delightful sharp-sweet smell which wafted to his nostrils even more strongly now as Histrina wallowed about in the flower's throat. A warm desirous feeling was rising in him, further stimulated by the sounds coming from within the lavender orchid some tens of yards away. Any resistance he might have had quickly evaporated.

He clambered up, gripping the lips of the slit and hauling himself inside as he had seen Histrina do.

They were in a fair-sized cavity, amply lit by the light sifting through the translucent walls of petal flesh. The floor was carpeted with a kind of thick fleecy pile, from which clouds of pollen rose with every tread. Near the walls the carpet sprouted big penis-like stamens which also ended in pollen dispensers. The effect was to drench them both in pollen every time they moved.

The sensation of actually being inside a flower was delightful, but there was scarcely time to savour a feeling so delicate, for the smell of the orchid was now overwhelming. Laedo had already guessed what the plant did. It released human pheromones, airborne chemicals which brought on an irresistible sexual urge. Histrina grabbed him as soon as he was inside, impatiently tugging at his clothing, of which he was just as anxious to divest himself. They went down together, rolling on the pollen mat, blood pounding, gasping with eagerness.

It seemed to Laedo that the whole globular chamber was banging like a drum to the beating of his heart. He had never known anything like it, not even in a pleasure house. Somewhere he could hear an uncontrolled roaring and wailing, both a man's voice and a woman's, and he completely failed to realize, at first, that it was his and Histrina's voices he was hearing.

How long did it go on for? He couldn't tell. He was submerged in his urges; there was no time. But eventually, after slaking his desires more deeply than he would have thought possible, he recovered his senses somewhat. He was lying on the floor of the orchid, arms still clasped around Histrina.

The gun lay a few feet away.

Only that forced him to clear his head. Otherwise he would probably have gone on, reaching plateau after plateau. He disentangled himself, casually picked up the gun, then wrapped it in his strewn clothing.

"Come on," he said huskily, "let's get back outside . . . for a while."

They stood up, and each laughed to see the other. Skin and hair were golden, dusted and shining. Still chuckling, Histrina bent to scoop up her gown.

Then she looked around for the gun, a frown crossing her features. Laedo forced himself quickly through the opening and lowered himself to the ground, then walked away at a steady pace.

Some distance away a man and a woman were standing looking up at the projector station. They were the same two, as far as Laedo could tell, who had entered the lavender orchid. Histrina caught up with him. He turned so as to keep his face to her. She seemed upset, furious, in fact—dangerously so. But, as long as he had the gun . . .

Placatingly he smiled. "That was great, wasn't it?"

"Give it back to me," she said in a hard voice.

He ignored her. "There are no insects here," he mused, looking up at the jungle, then at the sky. "No animals, no birds. Only people. The flowers use us to fertilise themselves with. That's why they're so big."

It was a marvellous piece of adaptation. Elsewhere it would have betokened an interesting line in selective evolution. On this planetoid, of course, the case was a little different. The orchids hadn't evolved quite by themselves. A guiding intelligence had given them a hand, or so he imagined—the intelligence of Klystar.

"*Give me my gun,*" Histrina said in a low, controlled

screech.

"It isn't your gun," Laedo said calmly. "It's mine, and I'm keeping it."

"Give it to me, you—" Histrina flew at him, snatching at the bundle of clothing under his arm, kicking and scratching.

"Stop it!" he bellowed. Putting out a hand to fend her off, he placed it squarely on a voluminous breast, and pushed her away.

Panting, she stopped, to stare over his right shoulder. Cautiously he turned. The other couple had strolled up. They were smiling a greeting.

"Haven't you finished?" the man said pleasantly. "You should have stayed in the bell."

"We have finished, actually," Laedo murmured. He inspected the two, interested to think they were the same whose ecstatic cries he had heard earlier. They were perfect physical specimens. The man was also undeniably handsome, and the woman beautiful. Quite obviously they were accustomed to their nakedness and had no use for clothing of any sort. They moved with a natural gracefulness, and radiated an air of unabashed friendliness.

Pure children of nature, he told himself. He was reminded of legends of man before the Fall. Something else they radiated was the sweetish odour of orchid pollen, an odour which he realized also surrounded Histrina and himself. The yellow dust clung to them all over, drenching the hair of head and genitals and adding a golden patina to the skin. Histrina, he noted, was eyeing the man up and down and was evidently excited by him. For his part, he found it hard to keep his eyes off the woman. Desirable though Histrina's body was, he had to admit that the other female surpassed her in comeliness.

"I haven't seen you two before," the woman said in a warm contralto. "Are you from another region?"

"We come from another world altogether," Laedo told her. He pointed to the bulking projector station. "We came in that. It's a spaceship, of sorts."

They glanced back at the station. "So that's what it is," the man said. He and the woman cooed, as though at something surprising, but then turned to Laedo again. Their lack of genuine astonishment was, to Laedo's mind, itself astonishing.

"Will you stay here long?" the man said.

"Some time, perhaps. It depends."

The woman spoke again, looking speculatively at Laedo. "Do you have flowers on your world?"

"Flowers? No, not the sort you have here. Only tiny ones." He demonstrated with his hands.

She pulled a face, as a child might. "I think I'd rather be here on Erspia."

"Erspia?"

"There you are!" Histrina said furiously to Laedo. "I *told* you this was Erspia!"

Laedo lowered his head towards her. "But it *isn't* Erspia," he insisted quietly.

"Oh yes, this is Erspia," the planetoid woman said brightly. "It's always been Erspia. What's the name of the world you come from?"

"Erspia!" Histrina said triumphantly.

Laedo sighed. "Look, it's only the name that's the same," he explained to Histrina. "Klystar must have given the one name to both worlds." He addressed the woman again. "Is there a being called Klystar on this world, by any chance?"

"Klystar?" She looked puzzled. "No, I don't think so."

The man looked at him with a new respect. "You speak of the great gardener," he said gravely. "He who created the garden of Erspia and placed us in the midst of it. No, he doesn't live here himself. He lives in heaven." He glanced back quickly at the projector station, a new thought seeming to strike him. "Can your spaceship go to heaven?"

Histrina laughed shortly.

The man laughed too, sharing her amusement even though ignorant of its cause. "My name is Lallalo," he said, making it sound musical, almost a snatch of song. "And this is Lila. What are you called?"

Laedo told him, and Lallalo smiled. "Well, we'll see you again, perhaps. Call on us before you leave."

Unconcernedly the pair strolled away.

"Wait!" Histrina cried. "Where are you going? Take us with you!"

She was animated, excited. They looked back, and smiled. Histrina hurried after them.

There were several other matters that Laedo thought he ought to be attending to. But his curiosity was too great, and after a few moments he, too, followed after the innocent dwellers in the garden of Erspia-2.

THREE

Laedo's Seduction

Two main problems, Laedo believed, faced him. And they each divided themselves into two sub-problems, one practical, one ethical.

The first problem concerned his line of business. Laedo was a cargo carrier. He had a small, fast ship, and specialised in carrying small, valuable cargoes. Space being so large and so easy to get lost in, such a carrier had not only to be highly skilled but also trustworthy to the point of saintliness.

In short, his main qualification was an ethical one. Accordingly, Laedo was highly ethical. He had undergone lengthy analysis in the *karmayoga*, or right action, school of psychotherapy. He had a certificate from his analyst which, in effect, gave him a moral rating. The certificate also stated that he had been attracted to the karmayoga school of psychology by reason of innate qualities, not because it might get him a special cargo carrier's ticket.

There was no other way to become a class CCC special-cargo carrier.

In other circumstances Laedo might have been more than willing to spend a considerable length of time on Erspia-2. It was a delightful place. But as it was he was bound, almost regretfully, to bend his efforts to an early departure—not just because to act otherwise would prejudice his chances of future employment, but because it was his duty. In his cargo strongroom were three kilograms of crystalline cavorite—the only known substance in the universe not to respond to inertial fields such as gravitation. It was worth half a billion *psalters,* and he was already months overdue.

So far he had accomplished the easier part of his task. He had found his ship in the jungle, already engulfed in luxurious, fast-growing vegetation. The hull was dented, but otherwise the tough little vessel checked out unharmed. Again using the manoeuvring engine, he had raised it and steered it to the clearing where the projector station lay. With the help of the ship's dog-sized and not-too-bright handling robot, he had clamped it in place on the station, from which it now stuck out at an odd angle.

But, worried about losing his ship again, he had taken the cavorite from the strongroom and hidden it in the projector station.

The hard part was to gain control over the projector station's drive.

Mulling over this, Laedo sat on the grass in the shadow of a saffron-coloured orchid shot through with pale blue, in whose bell he and Histrina slept at night. Nearby other orchids towered, creating the usual varicoloured fairyland. These orchids formed a grove in the middle of the meadow, separated from the main expanse of the jungle and nearer to the lake of fresh, cool water.

Totally incurious as to why the newcomers were here, Lallalo and Lila had willingly introduced them to the society of Erspia-2 if society it could be called. The inhabitants of the planetoid lived scattered like woodland animals throughout the jungle, mostly in small groups, though they tended to wander a good deal. They were as simple as children, and their lives were purely idyllic. They did no work, and had no unfulfilled desires: the orchids supplied all their needs. There were orchids in which to have unbelievably delicious fornication. There were orchids in which to sleep at night or, if one wished, to shelter from the occasional warm rain (though Laedo and Histrina, who by now had dispensed with all clothing, preferred to expose their bodies naked to the downpour). There were orchids whose interiors produced various kinds of foods—a sweet bread-like substance flavoured with honey; pulpy fruit-like growths; crunchy stalks with an endless variety of flavours, and so forth—and orchids in whose bells could be found petal-shaped bowls and pools of refreshing, invigorating drinks, coloured, flavoured and sometimes effervescent.

And there were orchids which offered food, drink, pheromonic fornication and a bedchamber all rolled into one.

Always the orchids deposited pollen on the people who entered them—which they mostly did for sexual purposes. The big flowers all differed subtly in the quality of their pheromones, so that sex in a new one was rather like sex with a new person.

Consequently people varied their copulating places a great deal—which was all part of the orchids' reproductive strategy, of course.

Sex, in fact, was mainly what the people of Erspia-2 occupied themselves with. Everyone was almost permanently dusted with golden pollen, except early in the morning when a bath in fresh water was the custom.

Laedo found it amusing to see how the orchids had incorporated human sexuality into their reproductive function. There were children on Erspia-2 also, but the birthrate was clearly very low. He had seen only three or four youngsters, while he had encountered hundreds of adults.

And not one of them but was superb from the physical point of view. Laedo had indulged himself to excess, for the people here were wholly promiscuous and never refused an offer of love play. But he never went to an orchid with a native woman if Histrina was around. Although she herself coupled quite openly with practically every man she met, she became insanely jealous whenever Laedo showed an interest in anyone but her.

Histrina.

Histrina was his second problem.

Knowing that she would eventually find an opportunity to get the gun back off him, he had hidden it in the station along with the cavorite. But he felt uneasy whenever she was near. He knew she wasn't sane, and that she would do anything which, in her imprinted condition of comic-book evil, seemed to her wicked. She would cheat, lie, steal, injure and murder. He felt, however, that he was safe from her violence for the time being. She needed him, or thought she did.

He was hoping that sating herself in fornication, which she also believed was unforgivably wicked, would keep her busy for the time being. But what was he going to do with her in the long run?

The simplest course seemed to be to leave her behind on Erspia-2. After all, she was having a good time.

But to some extent he was responsible for her condition. Although he had rescued her from Hoggora's camp, it was he who had flown her through the Ahrimanic beam at full intensity. Indeed, by bringing her aboard at all, he had wilfully taken her into his charge.

He could just imagine what his *karmayoga* analyst would say on hearing that he had abandoned his protegé. "This is bad, Laedo," he would say, shaking his head. "You're going to suffer agonies of remorse for this. You can expect to pay for it in other ways, too, through events in later life. You took on a load of bad karma when you ditched that poor girl."

No, she had to go with him. It was his duty to find some therapy that could straighten out that twisted mind of hers.

An idea occurred to him. What if he were to subject her to the Ormazdian beam at full intensity? Might that wipe out the Ahrimanic influence? It would be easy to switch the beam back on again and inveigle Histrina into it.

As a solution it was too clumsy, he decided. He wasn't a therapist, and the ploy might do more damage than good. Besides, he wasn't sure a Histrina oozing Ormazdian goodness wouldn't be even more insufferable than the one he had now.

He rose, stretched and sighed, partly with happiness at the sight of his surroundings and partly from a feeling of resignation at the thought or the task ahead. Sorting out the station's command system was going to be tricky.

Crossing the meadow, he entered the orchid forest, making for the globe of the station which bulked over the tips of the giant flowers, with the up-pointed cargo ship attached. Once in the forest he passed a group of Erspians who were lounging on the grass, chatting and laughing in silvery, musical voices. Receiving winsome smiles, he smiled back and went on.

Despite the planetoid's other attractions, if he were to stay here he would get pretty short of intelligent conversation after a while, he told himself. These people just didn't have developed minds. There was nothing to make them extend themselves.

A little further, and he come to the clearing where the station rested. He was about to mount the steep stairway to the hatch when he saw a woman standing under one of the nearest orchids. She was beckoning to him.

He peered. Even by Erspian standards, she was stunning. Her skin seemed to glow with health, a pink colour. Her golden hair shone; her mouth was vivacious and red.

He moved a little closer, and saw that there was no pollen on her. She hadn't had sex today yet. She was, quite obviously, eager for it.

Laedo licked his lips. He ought to be getting on with the job he had set himself. But by the habits of this world, one didn't refuse . . . besides, he hadn't had sex today himself yet.

And she was something he just couldn't pass up.

As he nodded and came up to her she smiled, her eyes sparkling. She turned and stepped into the jungle.

He had expected her to choose a nearby orchid but no, she went deeper into the forest, stepping soundlessly on the soft pile underfoot. He caught up with her and tried to take her hand. Her skin was cool; but she drew the hand away and kept her distance. Several times he spoke to her but she made no reply, merely gave him a sidelong glance and a heart-stirring smile of promise.

Pleasurably aware of the female motions of her rolling hips as she walked, he allowed her to lead him. The jungle surrounded them, the variegated shapes of the towering orchids offering endless vistas, the entrancing colours filtering the sunlight and filling the air with their hues.

He was unsure how long they walked; perhaps fifteen minutes. But suddenly she stopped and turned to him.

He was surprised that she still had not selected an orchid. He had thought to himself that perhaps she knew of a special one and that he was in for a rare treat. Instead she reached out her arms for him, and to his puzzlement seemed to want to make love on the ground.

Her lily-cool skin touched him; her arms went around his neck. She sank down, drawing him with her.

Her arms tightened more firmly around his neck. Her legs went around his upper thighs and clamped there.

And then the nightmare unfolded. The girl's skin was not human skin. Her flesh was not human flesh. It was composed of pulpy vegetable matter, and now it split down the middle, both body and head, to form a pod into which her arms and legs proceeded to press him.

Inside the pod he glimpsed pale finger-like extrusions, limp fronds, lumpy transparent growths which reminded him of jellyfish. He felt a stinging sensation as some of these fingers touched his skin. He yelled in fear and tried to push himself away, but the arms and legs were too strong; they were steadily squeezing him deeper into the pod, which with a creaking sound adjusted and extended itself to accommodate him. With a shock of panic he realized that it meant to close up again with him inside—after which he would no doubt be slowly digested.

He exerted himself to prise apart the lips of the almost imperceptibly closing pod. It was like trying to move an oak tree. Of course! he thought with bitter despair. Its only prey were human beings—naturally it was stronger than they were! His struggles became desperate and violent. He was gasping with fright.

Then he heard a hiss and felt a wave of heated air by his cheek. The head section of the pod blackened, shrivelled and peeled back. Suddenly the whole thing sprang open, pod agape, arms and legs akimbo.

He sprang to his feet, breathing heavily. His rescuer was Histrina. She had crept up unseen, his gun in her hand. A grimace of delight was on her features as, now, she directed the beam of the gun at the pod again, playing it up and down the horrible predator. Blackened and crackling, it squirmed and popped. It banged and hissed as fluid sacs within it exploded. Then it was a stinking mass which did no more than curl and uncurl slightly, giving off wisps of black smoke.

How had she got the gun back? He thought he had it well hidden.

Clever Histrina. She had done it again.

And this time he could not help but be emphatically glad of it. He looked down at his body. It bore a dozen or more red weals where the pod's stings had touched him, but he could no longer feel them. He brushed his chest and belly with his hand. He was numb.

Much longer, and he would no doubt have been completely paralysed.

So Erspia-2 wasn't a complete paradise after all, he thought dully. Predatory mimicry. A motile predator plant that used sexual enticement to trap its victims. What an apt variation on the orchid theme! And the pod had looked so perfectly like a woman!

Probably there were man-mimicking plants too. How did the biology of it work, he wondered? Plants generally did not collect enough energy to work a muscular system, but that did not necessarily apply to predator plants, of course. The disguised pod could gain enough energy from a human body to enable it to walk about for a while. Probably there were fat reservoirs where the energy was stored.

Then why hadn't these fat reserves flamed up in the heat of the gun's beam? Because, he reasoned, they were nearly exhausted. It had been time for the pod to claim another victim.

But why hadn't the Erspians warned him and Histrina about these predators? Perhaps they didn't even know about them. Perhaps they were just too simple-minded to draw the obvious conclusion when people went missing and skeletons were then found in the flower forest . . . if the pods left skeletons. Like animals that had lived long periods in safe environments, they had had all sense of danger bred out of them.

He wondered if the predators had been created along with the garden planetoid, or if they had evolved subsequently. The process of natural evolution might have been accelerated; a hangover of whatever process had been used to produce the orchids . . .

Still in a state of semi-shock, he came out of his ponderings to find Histrina now pointing the muzzle of the gun at him. Her eyes gleamed. She was revelling in the power she had over him—a power legitimised by the fact that she had saved his life.

"I ought to do the same to you!" she said shrilly. "You were going to go with her — with *that!*" She gestured hurriedly with the gun. "You're unfaithful to me!"

"But, Histrina," he said wearily. "What about you? You go with . . . anyone."

His voice fell to a mumble. What was the use? Wasn't it always the same? The thief was just as upset and indignant as anyone else if he was robbed. The thug and bully demanded that others respect his person.

Histrina had been brought up to regard sexuality in the strictly possessive sense. She delighted in breaking this moral rule herself, but she jealously demanded its strict observance in him, even though they were not formally married and, therefore, were in a state of damnation by her creed.

"You've been doing it with *others,* too!" she accused. "But I've fixed them! Come on, I'll show you!"

She let her gun hand fall and walked back the way she had come. Passively, Laedo followed.

She didn't go in the direction of the projector station, but somewhat to the left. She walked unfalteringly. Histrina had a good sense of direction.

After a few minutes she glanced about her, cast him a mischievous grin, and stopped by the stem of an orchid whose colour was a gorgeous apricot. "I'll show you later what I did," she said coyly. "There's something else I want you to see first. This orchid's different from the others."

Its bulb, or bell, was rather like a vast, nearly closed-up, apricot-hued tulip. The entrance was a circular portal through which one could crawl without having to push it apart any further. She went in on her hands and knees. While her fleshy buttocks were still in view her voice floated back to him. "I found it yesterday. Come and see."

Resignedly he obeyed. Once through the portal he rolled to the floor of the orchid and, as so often in recent days, found himself in an entrancing interior.

The very air glowed a warm apricot. The orchid's pheromones, however, seemed very weak. He felt little arousal at all. He decided, on reflection, that it was probably him who was at fault. He was still in a state of shock after his experience, or—more likely—the numbing effect of the pod's stings overrode the orchid's chemical sexual stimulation.

The floor of the orchid was uneven. From it, on mounds, there rose four fleshy stalks, ranging in height from one foot to two feet.

They were perfect-seeming replicas, if a trifle over-large, of the human phallus.

Histrina was on her knees caressing one of them, rubbing it up and down, holding it against her cheek. The glans was uncovered, and purple.

"It's *wonderful,*" she announced, leering up at him. "Come and feel."

He was reluctant, but she reached forward to seize his hand and drew him close, placing his fingers against the staff of the vegetable penis. It was less cool than he had expected. It was not as hot as an erect human penis could be, either. But it was warm. And somehow thrilling.

She let him take his hand away. He retreated and relaxed on his haunches to watch her play with the thing. She had it in both hands and was becoming more engrossed, her lips puckered as if she were murmuring and cooing to it.

Then her mouth went down on the purple knob, taking it all in, her head working up and down while her hands continued to perform similar motions down the shaft. He could hear her breath snorting through her nostrils.

Suddenly she convulsed, as if struck a physical blow. After a moment or two she removed her mouth and turned away from the penis, releasing it. She knelt there, eyes half closed. From her sullen, parted lips a golden syrup dripped. She let it run down her chin and drip to her breasts. Then she gathered it up and transferred it back to her mouth in gobs, rolling it round and round, swallowing it, licking her fingers and finally her smeared lips.

"Oh, it's delicious," she sighed.

She hadn't finished yet. She stood up and straddled the phallus, then lowered herself into a half-squatting position, jockeying herself over the purple glans. At first she seemed to have difficulty getting it in.

"It's big," she said breathlessly. "Aaaaaaahh!"

Once the phallus entered, Laedo was fascinated to see how deeply she could take the round purple knob into herself. Her eyes rolled up. Using the strength of her legs, she began to bounce up and down with increasing speed and eagerness. Her arms were waving in the air. She had retrieved the gun from where she had lain it when playing with the phallus and was holding it in her right hand. Laedo was nervous that she might start shooting wildly in her delirium.

"Aaaaahh," she breathed. "Aaaaaahh, aaaahh, *aaaarrghh!*"

The orchid chamber shook as if experiencing orgasm. Her chest heaved. Raising herself, she stood with eyes closed, as if reciting a mental prayer. The same golden syrup as before seeped from her and ran down her legs, so copiously that at first he thought she was thoughtlessly urinating.

She opened her eyes, as though suddenly recovering her senses, and looked at him. "There's one for you too," she said calmly. "Look."

Directing his attention to the apricot wall, she showed him a bulge and a cleft in the petal stuff, at about the height of a urinal tube in a men's room. Prising aside fleshy lips, she revealed an orifice.

"It does things," she said. She inserted a finger, then all four fingers, and seemed to be experiencing something interesting.

"Go on, you do it," she suggested, removing her fingers.

He put in his own fingers. The orifice was warm, warmer than the phallus had been, and moist. He felt a sucking, toying motion. Quickly he withdrew his hand.

"Go on, then," she urged impatiently, seeing him just stand there. "Stick it in!" She grabbed his penis and tried to tug it towards the cleft, but he stepped back and shook his head.

"No, I don't want to. I don't feel like it."

"You're just no fun at all," Histrina said disdainfully. She went down on her knees and wedged the gun between her thighs for safekeeping. She used the fingers of one hand to prise apart the lips of the orchid vulva, and the other to guide her breast to the orifice. Her distended nipple went in. She pushed and squirmed and squeezed until, finally, the breast itself was lodged halfway in the organ, the visible part swollen and tight-skinned as she pressed it as hard as she could against the vulva.

Laedo could see the breast surging under the action of the orchid vagina.

Appreciatively Histrina was going, "Mmmmmm, mmmm-mm . . . "

He had seen enough. He crawled out of the bell and sat on the grass, waiting for Histrina to finish.

Listening to her murmurs of pleasure from within, a horrifying thought struck him.

Was what he had seen simply a variant of the orchids' usual technique for obtaining a pollen carrier—or was it another, slower form of predation? What was the function of the syrup the vegetable penis had ejaculated? Was it addictive?

Or had the orchid ejected fertilised seed into Histrina, who would now become a doomed seed-bed?

He took his head in his hands and groaned.

She dropped lightly and gaily from the bell a few minutes later. Her breath and loins, he noticed, smelled sweet.

"That was great," she congratulated herself. "Come on, and I'll show you the other thing. It will be a lesson to you."

Able to summon no will of his own, he followed.

She took him to a place he recognised. It was a glade in the jungle, not far from the grove where he and Histrina lived, and not far from the projector station either, though that was not visible from here, surrounded as they were by orchids.

The previous day Laedo had visited the glade, and had had sex sessions with several of the women there.

The scene which now met his eyes was less inviting. Half a dozen men, and three women, stood surrounding three female forms which lay limply on the grass. Those standing gave Histrina peculiar, puzzled stares which she ignored. Smiling knowingly, she invited Laedo to take a look at the women on the ground, pointing with her gun.

With a feeling of dread he eased himself through the group. Three girls. Each with a hole burned neatly in her forehead.

They were three out of the four women Laedo had copulated with the day before.

"See?" Histrina said primly. "That's what's going to happen every time you're unfaithful to me. I saw what you were up to here yesterday—you dirty beast! I followed you and hid behind an orchid. I would have done for them there and then, but I didn't find the gun till this morning. Then, just as I'd finished and was coming back to the station, I saw you going off with that other bitch! Only she wasn't a bitch, was she?" she added thoughtfully. "She was some kind of *thing.*"

In spite of how sick he felt, Laedo was able to ask, "You killed them—right here?"

"Yes. Went up to them, put the gun to their heads, and—poof! Down they went!" She broke into a fit of giggles, demonstrating by poking the gun at the air. "And do you know what? Nobody did a damned thing about it!"

He wondered how she had missed seeing him copulate with the fourth girl. Then he remembered that she had also found the new kind of orchid yesterday. She must have wandered off at some point.

The Erspians were paying no heed to their conversation.

"They're not going to get up," a girl said.

"No," a man said gravely. "They're finished."

"Come on, then," said another, nudging a corpse tentatively with his foot. "We'd better take them where they belong."

What followed was the nearest thing to organised collective labour Laedo had yet seen on Erspia-2. The men arranged themselves two to a dead girl. One stepped between the corpse's legs and lifted it with his arms behind the knees. The other lifted it by the arms.

Awkwardly the procession went off through the jungle. The females stayed behind. They lay down, lounged and chewed grass. They showed no sign of distress over the sudden deaths of their friends, though occasionally they glanced worriedly at Histrina

Laedo was curious to see whether any ceremony would attend the disposal of the bodies, or if they would simply be left lying somewhere. Quietly he followed the party. They didn't go far, only about fifty yards, to halt before a cream-coloured, capsule-shaped orchid bell he had vaguely noticed before. It had no visible mouth and hung close to the ground on its stem. It looked, he thought, almost fungoid.

The leader dropped his burden, still leaving his partner holding the dead girl up by her knees. He cupped his hands to his mouth and let out a high-pitched musical tone which wavered, like the ringing of a bell.

In answer the orchid promptly opened up a gaping maw which ran its entire length. With a shudder Laedo saw that its interior resembled, not a little, the inside of the girl-mimicking pod that had trapped him, except that this was much, much bigger.

Big enough, in fact, not just for three bodies but for twice that number, had they been present. Wordlessly the work party took hold of the cadavers one by one, by wrists and ankles, swung them once, then tossed them into the bell of the waiting orchid.

That was it. No ceremony, no farewell. The orchid closed again with a crunch, and the men set off back the way they had come, giving Laedo vague but friendly smiles as they passed.

He turned and bumped into Histrina, who without his knowing it had followed him. "Just what is it," he said in a low, angry tone, "that makes you think you can murder whoever you like whenever you like?"

She stared at him as though he were mad. "What are you worrying about them for? They deserved to die. They were wicked."

"These people? How can you call *them* wicked?"

"Because they *sin*. They do it all the time." Her eyes widened. "In the orchids. That's just as bad as killing people, the priest at home says."

Laedo saw that she believed what she was saying. She was not joking. Before he could frame a reply she continued, speaking waspishly. "It's terrific here, Laedo. Do you see what these people are like? They're just like little children—naughty children, but quite helpless. You can do anything you like with them. We're going to be their king and queen. They'll all be our slaves, every one, and do our bidding."

"I thought you wanted to go on to Harkio," Laedo reminded her wearily.

"Yes!" she said passionately, and her words came in a rush. "We'll do everything we want to do here and then we'll go to Harkio and do everything we want to do there!"

The will-numbing effect of the pod's poison must have worn off. At any rate Laedo know what he had to do, and he did it quickly. He stepped to Histrina, kneed her in the solar plexus, and jabbed his fist at her jaw as she doubled up and dropped the gun. She reeled and sprawled stunned to the ground.

Wrestling her over his shoulder, he stooped to retrieve the gun, and then he was off through the orchid jungle towards the projector station. She began to stir as he was clambering up the stairway, making him wonder if he had hit her hard enough, but she didn't struggle.

He withdrew the stairway, closed the hatch, and made for the control room. Dropping her in a corner, he activated the board. The viewscreen lit up, showing the ground hanging aslant the from top of the screen, upended by the angle of the station's inner floors.

He looked at Histrina, who was conscious now and had sat up. "Just stay there, and don't move or you'll get the same again," he warned her.

She nursed her jaw and stared at him sulkily.

Laedo addressed the hidden controller. "We've been trying to report to Klystar," he said. "But he isn't on this world any more. He's left. Hand control of the station over to me."

Chatter-chatter-chatter. Parchment shuddered from the machine and floated floorward.

Must report to Klystar, the burned-in words read simply. A light came on, showing that the drive unit had been energised.

There was a slight swaying sensation which was probably visual in origin, for the scene on the viewer swivelled to make the ground a vertical wall. The station had righted itself.

The drive acted in a direction parallel to the floor, in the same manner as on a surface or ocean vessel. The horizon slid away and vanished. In an amazingly short time, the planetoid's atmosphere thinned and became black space thick with stars.

Erspia-2 dwindled.

Laedo slumped in one of the control board's two chairs, asking himself if he had really thought this thing through. His main concern had been to get Histrina sway from the planetoid before she started killing again. His hope that he could actually persuade the station to give him control of the drive was, he realized, forlorn.

"*Now* where are we going?" he wondered out loud.

But this time, the machine didn't answer.

FOUR

War of the Worlds

Gauzewing and her lover Flit would delight to make love in the orchards and in the bowers, and in the scented pools and wild woods, but most of all in the air, which was where they disported now, wings beating in time together as they flew at a leisurely pace through fluffy cloud and emerged into flashing sunlight. Pivoting on the breeze, Flit seized his sweetheart. They hovered with bodies pressed close together, wings quivering, squeezing in rhythmic ecstasy. Then, the final rapture spent, they parted to go tumbling and spinning like sycamore seeds, recovering to soar and dip just above the level of the treetops.

Flit alighted on a bough which presented itself like an elegantly extended hand in the roof of the forest. Gauzewing joined him and they sauntered to the cushioned pad of a giant green leaf. There they lay down and nestled together, gazing overhead.

It was always a fascinating sight. First, easily within flying distance, were scuds of fluffy cumulus. Far, far higher, looming over everything like a vast roof, was the upper world, with its rivers, its mountains, its seas and green plains, all upside down.

The upper world had its own clouds, too, which appeared to crawl over its surface, small and white. Often they seemed to merge with the larger clouds of the lower world, creating a criss-cross movement.

Gauzewing averted her eyes, resting her head on Flit's shoulder. The upper world was awesome, but menacing. At night tiny flares and spots of light could be seen. These were said to be fires which the denizens of the upper world, the gnomes, used to smelt metals from ores they dug out of the ground in deep tunnels, and to make all their fiendish contraptions, such as the catapults with which they flung rocks to the lower world to try to wreak havoc. There had been none of the bombardments lately. When they began again, the fairy folk would know the gnomes were preparing to come parachuting down in another of their attempted invasions.

Hazily she watched as, approaching from the distance, a troupe of men-fairies came flying in formation, bearing spears and bows. For a while they wheeled about, practising stabbing with their spears and shooting arrows. All men regularly had to spend a few hours training in the militia, in case the gnomes came back. But their manoeuvres were half-hearted. Soon they would descend into the foliage to lounge and rest.

Then Gauzewing jerked her head up and stared in shock. Beyond the flying warriors, soaring swiftly on, came a huge round shape. It glinted in the light of the two suns, clearly made of metal. She had never seen anything like it, and as it neared it swelled and swelled, growing huger and huger.

She trilled a scream. "Gnomes! Gnomes!"

Flit was staring too. He seemed paralysed. Overhead the militia, responding to the orders of their sergeant, whose voice floated down faintly, turned to face the monster. But their nerve soon deserted them, and they fled.

Laedo, when the projector station came in sight of what he came to think of as Erspia-3, screwed up his eyes in astonishment.

The planetoid was like a split pea, divided right through its equator. The two hemispheres were poised in space, separated by about ten miles.

He had little time to study the phenomenon in detail, because the station was already sailing into the gap. Two immense flat landscapes were revealed, each inverted in relation to the other. Standing on either, one would see an upside-down land in the sky. Laedo thought of the ancient fairy-tale of Jack the Giant-Killer.

His respect for the engineers of the planetoid cluster—or engineer, if it really was the work of a single being—increased still further. Whoever had sculpted Erspia-3 was supreme in the use of inertial fields, able to keep the two halves of this world in position by means of invisible pillars of force.

The projector station had selected one of the two landscapes and was skimming below what now became the 'lower' cloud layer. A lush Eden spread out before Laedo's gaze. It was a little reminiscent of Erspia-2, but with less colour. These were not orchid forests, but verdant woods with immense, spreading trees.

"I wonder if there are people here," Histrina murmured, looking over his shoulder.

"We'll find out soon, I imagine. If there are, you had better behave yourself!"

He frowned. A flock of birds, or some other flying creatures, had appeared ahead. He blinked. For a moment they looked almost like flying humans. Then they appeared to become startled and flew off.

A mass of treetops approached. The station gyrated, swerved, then made for a clearing through which there ran a silvery stream. It was effecting a more controlled landing than it had managed on Erspia-2. Gently, with hardly a bump, it set down right way up.

"No need to check the air," Laedo murmured. "There *will* be people around somewhere. All these worlds have been designed for human habitation."

"People . . . " Histrina echoed greedily. She licked her lips.

"I told you to behave yourself!" Laedo snapped. "I won't stand for any more of your crazy behaviour!"

She pouted. "But I want to have *fun.*"

"Don't we all." Laedo inspected the scenery on the viewscreen. The trees were gargantuan, much bigger than on Earth or Harkio. They were spacious, too. One seemed to be able to peer through the forest for an indefinite distance. The enormous boughs spread and intertwined in all directions, fit to make pathways through the air. The leaves looked pretty near large enough to bear a man's weight.

The 'sky' did not appear on the screen. Probably he could see it by raising the viewing angle, easily done by fiddling with the control slides, but he decided to reserve that pleasure for his first excursion outside. It must be quite a sight.

"You know something? I'll bet people round here live in the trees. They're big enough. I don't see any tree houses, though. Perhaps we're in an uninhabited part. Okay, Histrina, let's take a look outside."

He led the way to the hatch. This time there were no complications in reaching the ground. As soon as he opened the hatch the stairway extended itself.

They stood on the platform and gawped. Above them reared the 'sky', but it was not a sky. It was another landscape poised upside down, like a map stretched out overhead. The sight was stunning in its stupendousness but somehow not oppressive. After a while, Laedo thought, one might cease to become aware of the other terrain.

He studied the inverted world. Was it the same as this one? A mirror image, even? Widespread green swathes mostly covered it, also sparkling inland seas and wandering veins that could be rivers. There were also brown patches, deserts perhaps. He didn't recall seeing any of those on the approach to the lower world.

Cloud drifted over the upper landscape. It suddenly struck him that both worlds were in broad daylight. Peering through the encompassing forest, he was able to locate a small bright sun—presumably another artificial sun like those which lit Erspias 1 and 2. It sent down slanting rays from a position near the rim of the upper world.

Examining it carefully, noting the shallow angle of its rays, he realized that it was 'set' from the other world's point of view. It was not currently visible there at all.

Where, then, was the upper world getting its light from?

The question would have to wait. Stepping from the platform, Laedo descended the stairway. Once outside the station's resident gravity field he was surprised by an abrupt drop in body-weight. Experimentally he jumped off the step, to find himself floating slowly to the ground.

Evidently Erspia-3's gravity was maintained at only a fraction of Earth-normal. Why was that?

Behind him, Histrina was also experiencing reduced weight. To her, it was a complete novelty. It had merely puzzled her when she saw Laedo falling with the slowness of a leaf, and on stepping down the stairs the new sensation left her confused. Unlike Laedo she was not accustomed to walking in low gravity and she bounced along the turf like a balloon.

Turning to him, she laughed the laugh of a delighted child on some fairground amusement, jumping high in the air and giggling uncontrollably as she sedately descended.

Laedo smiled. "You walk like this, see?" He showed her how to step with sliding movements which did not send one rocketing upward. She quickly mastered the trick, but for the moment seemed more interested in leaping about with abandon.

Laedo meanwhile stood quietly gazing about him. The being or beings who had made the Erspia worlds had a real talent for it, there was no question about that. A forest of normal-sized oaks might look like this to a small animal such as a squirrel, he told himself. He saw no sign of animals of any kind, but one would not necessarily see animals in a Harkio forest straight away. Arboreal creatures were good at keeping out of sight.

He recollected the flying creatures he had seen. Peering up through the foliage, he squinted.

Here they came again.

A clarion call sounded through the aerial glades. Flit turned to Gauzewing, trying to put a look of courage on his delicate features.

"We are called to arms."

Both tilted their faces to the sky, searching for the tell-tale glints that would precede a gnome attack. So far, though, there was nothing to see. The gnome-world overhead glared at them balefully, but passively.

Perhaps the gnomes were trying something new.

"Go into the forest with the other women, Gauzewing," Flit ordered. "Wait until it's safe."

"Oh, let me come and see what happens," she implored. "I'll fly away quickly if there's fighting, I promise."

Flit knew he could not change her mind once she had come to a decision. "Stay to the rear, then," he said.

Then he was off, launching himself into the air and flying swiftly towards the armoury, past numerous tree-villages one would scarcely see unless one already knew they were there. He dipped under the forest cover until he came to the local military training camp.

The camp was unusual, for fairy habitations, in being on the ground. Gauzewing alighted on an overhead tree branch on the edge of the clearing, so slender it almost bent under her weight. Flit meanwhile fluttered to the entrance of the large storage hut.

In the glade there was an air of excitement. Other fairy men were descending on the clearing, consternation on their faces. A sergeant thrust a bow and quiver of arrows at Flit.

"Here, put these on. Did you see the strange object? It's landed somewhere by the Arn stream."

"Yes, I saw it. Are you sure it's from up above?"

"Where else would it be from? We don't make anything like that. Probably packed with a hundred gnomes. Let's make short work of them."

He ushered Flit out of the camp, together with everyone else who had been issued arms, to make way for the others who were arriving.

Flit found himself with the first troop to set out. They flew low over the tree cover. Glancing back, Flit spotted Gauzewing following at a distance, gliding from hiding place to hiding place in the treetops.

The clearing through which the Arn stream flowed came into view. And there was the huge, frightening gnome thing, bigger than any tree house, bigger even than the great lodges which spread over three trees or more for holding festive gatherings. Despite all the brave talk, the fairies did not launch themselves into an immediate attack. They flew round the edge of the clearing while the marshals discussed what to do.

Down below were two figures, who had presumably emerged from the giant round thing. One was jumping up and down, the other was simply gazing around as if in wonderment. The fairies had expected gangs of ferocious gnomes to come rushing out, killing everyone in sight, and the turn of events puzzled them.

Eventually the air marshal selected Flit and another trooper, Flutter, to take a closer look. Flit saw Gauzewing put her hands to her face in fright as she realized what was afoot, but he steeled himself to risk his life. He and Flutter swooped down, straight for the strangers.

The figure which had been jumping about stopped on noticing the fairies and stood staring at the surrounding troop with no apparent sign of alarm. Neither figure carried anything which looked like a weapon, which Flit also thought unusual. He and his comrade swooped so low towards the two that they could clearly see the expressions on their faces. Then their shimmering wings carried them up again to make their report.

"Well," barked the air marshal, standing on a winding bough, "are they gnomes?"

"Yes," said Flit.

"No," said Flutter at the same time.

The air marshal looked from one to the other.

"They must be gnomes," Flit insisted. "They don't have wings."

"They don't have wings," Flutter agreed, "but they are not gnomes. They look more like us." He glanced sidelong at Flit. "You can see they're not gnomes."

"What else can they be if they don't have wings?" Flit argued in puzzlement.

Once more the air marshal peered down into the clearing.

Suddenly Gauzewing was by their side. "I think one of them's a girl!" she proclaimed.

Before they could stop her she had spread her wings and was lunging fearlessly in a steep glide into the clearing. Pulling herself up sharp, she dropped her feet on the grass before the two visiting strangers.

Above her towered the metal wall of the strange flying building. She glanced at it only briefly, before looking directly into the faces first of the woman, then the man.

"Hello," she said.

Laedo was astounded.

They weren't birds, or bats, or flying reptiles.

They were people.

On first seeing them circling the clearing, Laedo had assumed them to be wearing nullgrav packs. He hadn't quite believed his eyes on sighting the shimmer of dragonfly-type wings. Only when two of their number descended into the clearing for a closer look, hurriedly returning to their perches, had he realized the truth.

A fair-sized number of the winged humans were looking down on them, and they all carried primitive weapons—spears, bows and arrows—causing Laedo's hand to go instinctively to the gun at his waist.

"Let's get back inside the station, Histrina," he said. He

didn't want to be alarmist, but a well-aimed arrow could kill as surely as a bullet or e-beam.

But the slim figure who came gliding down was empty handed, and her unthreatening demeanour checked his caution. With the lightness of a butterfly she set herself deftly on the grass, and smiled at them.

"Hello," she said, in a cool, friendly voice.

"Hello," Laedo answered.

"Why, she's a fairy!" Histrina exclaimed. "Only bigger."

"Yes, I'm a fairy," answered the flying girl innocently. "But what are you?"

They stared at her. She was small and slim, hardly bigger than a child of ten or eleven. A loose, silky garment partly concealed her body, caught at the waist by a braided cord. Her golden hair fell loosely to her shoulders. Her features were delicate.

Her gauzy iridescent wings were attached somewhere near her shoulder blades. There were only two of them—Laedo would have expected four, like a dragonfly's—and they were oval in shape. When not in use they came together behind her like the wings of a butterfly, though they did not touch.

"I am Gauzewing," the self-confessed fairy said.

Laedo smiled at the name. "I am Laedo. And this is Histrina."

Gauzewing pointed to the sky. "You are not from. . . ?"

Laedo glanced at the overhead landscape. "No, we are not from there. We are from a different world altogether."

She frowned, having difficulty with the concept. Then she indicated the fairy militia in the treetops.

"My friends think you are our enemies the gnomes."

She hesitated, then spoke again. "What happened to your wings?"

Now more of the strange inhabitants of this land were quitting the treetops and alighting beside Gauzewing, making Laedo uneasy. He noted that Histrina showed no fear. She was gleefully eyeing the winged men, though her glance went periodically back to Gauzewing.

"You see, they aren't gnomes," Gauzewing announced.

The first of the newcomers to land had placed a proprietorial hand on Gauzewing's arm. He made a perfect match for her, with his poetic features and a bow slung over his shoulder.

"Perhaps the gnomes have cut off their wings," he suggested.

"They do that, sometimes."

Watching the troop flutter down from the trees, one mystery was solved for Laedo. The fairies were the reason why Erspia-3's gravity was so low. It was to enable them to fly. Their moderately sized membrane wings would have been useless for carrying normal human body weight. Even then, the fairies were all small and light-boned. The tallest among them did not exceed five feet in height.

Klystar—if there was a Klystar—had designed the planetoid with the human fairies in mind. At the same time, he must have had the ability to redesign the human stock at his disposal genetically. Laedo did not see how the fairies' wings could have evolved naturally.

Glancing up, he saw yet more armed fairies arriving. Evidently the appearance of the station in this idyllic setting was cause for great alarm.

A spear-bearing individual, a leader of some sort by his bearing, pushed his way through to confront Laedo.

"Do you come from the gnome world?"

"You mean up there?" Laedo pointed. "No. We come from a different world altogether."

"There *are* only two worlds," the other said doubtfully. Then he shrugged. "Still, you are clearly not gnomes, and you do not belong to our race either. You are too tall."

He let his gaze rove over the towering space station. "Neither have I known the gnomes to make anything like this. How does it move through the air? There was no parachute."

"It's hard to explain." Nervously Laedo watched as Histrina moved close to one of the men fairies and began stroking his arm. He considered inviting one or two leading fairies into the station, then thought better of it. They might interpret it as an attempted capture. Besides, he did not know how to adjust the internal gravity, or even know if that was possible at all. The fairies would barely be able to stand up once they got inside.

"Histrina!" he said sharply. "Come over here."

With a sulky pout she obeyed him.

"My name is Laedo," he said to the spear-carrying fairy. "And this my companion is Histrina. What shall I call you?"

"I am called Highbreeze," the other replied, "and I am an air marshal of the defence militia. This one, who so bravely came down to meet you, though with reckless disregard for her own safety, is Gauzewing. And this is her companion Flit."

An ever-thickening flock of fairies was circling overhead. Laedo decided on a pacificatory gesture. "Let us talk," he said, and sat cross-legged on the grass, dragging Histrina down beside him, preferring to have her where she could get up to no mischief.

"You are wrong when you think there are only two worlds," he told Highbreeze, once he and half a dozen other fairies had followed his example. "There are other worlds far off, too far away for you to see. We come from one of those, in the . . . moving house you see behind me."

"Were you not actually here, that would be almost impossible to believe," Highbreeze commented. "Do you intend to stay with us long?"

"That depends."

Laedo pondered. "So you have a militia. You fight. There are wars between you?"

"Not between ourselves!" Highbreeze told him emphatically. "We are peaceful people who wish only to be left alone to enjoy our lives and raise our children. We are forced to fight to defend ourselves from the gnomes, who want to destroy us." He raised his eyes. "They live on that accursed world up there, and every so often attempt to invade us."

"Then it's possible to cross between the two worlds? Can you fly across the gap?"

Highbreeze shook his head. "No, it is not possible to fly that high. The gnomes, who have no wings and cannot fly at all, manage it because they are expert engineers. They hurl themselves away from their world by means of catapult machines, and once past the midpoint parachute down to us. They are not content with one world. They want two."

Laedo thought to himself that it might be interesting to visit the gnomes' world. They might have metal-workers who could make a better job of casting a transductor for his space-ship than had Hoggora's mechanic on Erspia-1.

"How do the gnomes get back home?" he asked curiously.

"They don't! We see to that!" boasted Highbreeze. "Except in the beginning, when we accorded them the status of guests and allowed them to build catapult machines for the return journey. Now that they are enemies all who come here have been killed or captured."

Having said that, he eyed Laedo thoughtfully. Laedo hastily reassured him.

"We have no unfriendly intentions towards you," he said. "We have lost our way and wish to go home, that is all. You must judge for yourselves whether we most resemble the gnomes or yourselves."

"It is true that you look like us, but on the other hand . . ."

Highbreeze rose and strolled to where the projector station rested. He touched the stairway, then stroked the silver-grey metal of the bulging hull.

"Fairies do not make metals," he said simply. "That is something gnomes do."

There was a stirring among the militiamen on hearing this.

"There are many worlds, with many different kinds of people," Laedo said hurriedly. "Many of them make metals. You can learn to do it yourselves if you wish. I can teach you."

While saying this he was measuring the distance to the projector station's entrance. The air marshal shook his head, then came back and sat down again.

"We are happy with our way of life."

The others relaxed.

Laedo said slowly, "Have you ever heard of someone called Klystar?"

No, the fairy folk had not heard of Klystar. Like the inhabitants of Erspias 1 and 2, they had no real knowledge of their origins.

It was the second day of their sojourn on the split planetoid. Laedo and Histrina lounged on the grass in front of the projector station, eating fruit the fairies had brought them.

A large insect, resembling a dragonfly, but three or four times the size, hummed past. Watching its shimmering wings, Laedo thought of the miraculous mutation wrought on the local humans. The design of their wings was somewhat like that of a dragonfly or damselfly. They did not beat as fast, of course—one could clearly see their sculling motion. Neither was there an ugly hump of muscle to power them, as one might have expected: just a tendon-like triangle near each shoulder blade which was barely noticeable.

By now he had been able to discern something of the mechanics of this world. Like the other Erspias it kept to a day of about twenty-eight hours, but unlike those, it had two suns, sharing the same orbit in diametric opposition to one another. That orbit was tilted with respect to the planetoid's sundered diameter, meaning that both suns shone through the gap at the same time, but from opposite directions. They also 'set' and 'rose' at roughly the same time, again in opposite directions.

The arrangement was neat. The prime reason for it, as far as Laedo could see, was that the suns were not visible at an elevation higher than about twenty-five degrees, and if there were only one of them there would always be long shadows. Presumably this was displeasing to the split world's designer. As it was, long shadows appeared for a short time in mornings and evenings, since the higher sun remained in line of sight for a brief period after the lower sun had set.

On the approach to Erspia-3 he had noticed that life was restricted to the two flat surfaces, and had not spread to the outsides of the hemispheres. That probably meant that they were bare to the void. The inertial fields which kept the hemispheres poised a few miles apart also hemmed in the air.

It was a tribute to 'Klystar's' ingenuity that the whole arrangement continued to work after a fairly long period of time. People spoke with slightly different accents on each of the three Erspias Laedo had visited, and from that he deduced that the worldlets had been set up at least a hundred years ago.

Just how many Erspias were there? And what was the reason for such an eccentric piece of world construction?

"Are we going to stay here?" Histrina asked lazily, tickling herself with a stalk of grass. "It's nice here, isn't it? And there are such *pretty* people."

"We may have to stay for a while, Histrina."

Until I figure out how to take control of the projector station's drive, or to fix my spaceship, he told himself in aggravation. He was going to have to keep close tags on Histrina. The flying folk were not the helpless children the people in the orchid forest were. They would retaliate if she harmed any of them.

He got to his feet. Over the gargantuan treetops a group of flyers came in sight. This time they carried no weapons. They glided gracefully down into the clearing, their wings sculling the air as they pulled up to set their feet on the ground with perfect skill.

There were six of them, including Gauzewing and Flit.

"You asked to see one of our gnome prisoners," Flit said.

Laedo nodded. He wanted to question a representative of this reputedly skilled race.

"The elders see no objection. However, wingless as you are . . ."

Two fairies unrolled a long mat which one of them had been carrying. It was made of wooden slats linked together, and was gaily coloured red and blue. At each corner was a thong. Four fairies stationed themselves one to a corner, placing a thong over one shoulder.

"It would take you a long time to walk to where the prisoner cages are," Flit said. "We will carry you on this litter. We use it for transporting sick and injured people."

Laedo blinked and swallowed as he imagined himself borne through the air on the flimsy mat. He tried to estimate the impact velocity if he tumbled from a height in this gravity. Still enough, he guessed, to cause death or serious injury.

Or would the fairies simply zoom down and catch him as he fell?

It was not something he cared to put to the test. "I don't have wings," he said, "but I *can* fly. Wait here for a minute."

Like any spaceship, the exterior of the projector station was studded with footholds and handrails. Laedo clambered up these until he came to the port of his cargo ship. Inside, he went to the equipment store room and found one of two gravpacks, strapping it to his back like a satchel.

Back at the port, he put a hand on the control knob on the chest strap and soared gently up and forward.

Flying with a gravpack was simplicity itself. The knob controlled the degree of 'lift' or inertial push, enabling one to rise or sink in a gravity field. To go forward, one leaned forward. To go back, one leaned back. To turn, one simply—turned.

Playfully he rotated, dipped and rose, showing off in front of the fairy people before setting himself down on the grass. They didn't seem as impressed as he would have thought, but simply shrugged and rolled up the litter again.

"I don't know how you do that, but very well," Flit said. He paused. "It's just as well the gnomes don't have anything like it. Our one big advantage over them is that we can fly and they can't."

"I doubt if they'll get that clever," Laedo responded.

Suddenly he noticed Histrina's reaction. The girl was enthralled. She didn't know about gravpacks, of course.

He turned to her. "Histrina," he said firmly, "I want you to stay here until I get back. I would prefer it if you stayed in the station, but in any case I don't want you to go wandering off. Do you understand?"

She pouted. "I want to come. Show me how to fly like you just did."

"There isn't another gravpack," Laedo lied. "Stay here, I won't be long."

He followed the fairies as they flittered into the air. It was easy to keep up with them. They flew with arms dangling and bodies aslant, much as he did. The enormous trees fell away below. From a height the forest canopy looked like a panorama of hills, dells and meadows, all covered in a frizzy moss. Here and there were clearings and glints of streams.

The fairies did not seem to tire as their wings bore them onward. They seemed able to fan their wings indefinitely. At length, they dipped, and as they neared the tree cover Laedo saw a cleft in the foliage which would not easily have been visible from higher in the air. Through this the flying party slipped, then went spearing and side-stepping among the boughs, making for the shadowed depths.

Soon they were on the ground, walking the bank of a rippling stream. Despite the size of the trees—or perhaps because of it—there was no gloom. Sufficient sunlight filtered through to dapple the forest floor with glowing, dancing spots.

A cave of branches opened up: not a clearing as such, but a domed hollow matted with boughs end foliage. Laedo wondered whether this was deliberate camouflage. Did the gnomes in the world above possess telescopes?

About a dozen cages were set in the hollow. In them, figures huddled. Flit led Laedo to the nearest one.

And so, for the first time, he saw a gnome.

An uglier creature was hard to imagine. The gnome was short, no taller then the fairies, but it was squat and round, almost ball-shaped, giving an impression of compact strength. It had bulbous, muscular limbs. Its naked skin was an angry red, as if it had been scalded, and was covered in warts. As for the face, with its bulging eyes and pointed ears, it was a fanged grimace.

The gnome clambered to his feet on seeing the two, and shook the bars of his cage with a defiant snarl, while along the line his fellows did the same.

Laedo hoped the cage was strong enough to withstand the creature's frustration. He stood pensively, thinking of what had been wrought to produce such a travesty of a human being. To think that human stock had been intentionally modified to produce this result displeased him.

Evidently Klystar had delved into human mythology to produce both fairies and gnomes. Traditionally the latter were miners and skilled metal-workers. For all their ugliness and ferocity, the gnomes could perhaps prove useful to him.

Politely he asked, "Do you have a name?"

The gnome replied in a thick, rasping voice.

"KILL ALL FAIRIES! THIS LAND WILL BE OURS!"

"Hmm," said Laedo.

Admittedly, it was not a promising start. He studied the leering face in front of him, and found that it was actually possible to discern a family resemblance with the fairies and with the other Erspians such as Histrina, despite the grotesqueness of that resemblance. It strengthened his belief that the Erspia worlds had been stocked from a relatively small number of original settlers.

Flit responded to the gnome's taunt with a superior smile, and wandered away to join his fellows.

Such innocence was touching. How could he be sure that Laedo was not, after all, in league with his enemies?

Laedo edged closer to the cage and caught a whiff of the

creature, a smell like rotten potatoes. He spoke quietly. "Look at me. You will see that I am not a fairy. My face is different. I am taller. I have no wings."

The gnome pulled a face and looked puzzled.

"If you're not a gnome you're a fairy," he grunted flatly.

Laedo let it pass. "Is it true you have good metal-workers in Gnomeland?" he asked. That was what the fairies called the upper world. "Can you make any shape in metal?"

Once again the gnome seemed to be puzzled by what Laedo was saying. "Yes!" he boasted finally. "We can make anything! We are not like those useless fairies who cannot make anything at all, except in wood, and do not deserve their world. There are metal ores here! They rightly belong to us!"

Despite their belligerence, Laedo began to sense a workmanlike intelligence in these squat, solid beings. Metal-work seemed to be an obsession with them.

It could be just what he needed.

He lowered his voice yet further, ducking his head.

"Don't repeat what I'm saying. Do you want to go back home?"

Suspicion and incomprehension glared from the gnome's bulbous eyes. "Uh?"

"Do your people know how to make *steel?*"

The gnome nodded.

"There's something I want made. I have nothing to do with the fairy folk. I come from a different world altogether—one you know nothing about. If I free you and return you to Gnomeland, can you get this thing made for me?"

The squat creature made no response to the talk of other worlds, if the idea penetrated his brain at all. He thought for a moment, then made a gesture to one side, swivelling his eyes.

"My comrades, too."

"I can't manage that," Laedo said. "I'm not even sure I can get you away."

"The fairies are returning," the gnome muttered, coming close to the bars of his cage. "If you do what you promise, then we shall see."

"Have you had enough of the ruffian?" Flit asked as he rejoined Laedo.

"I think so."

"I imagined it would take little to satisfy your curiosity. They are nothing but brutes."

Laedo had to admit his plan had dangers. He was basing his optimism on his experiences with Hoggora and his horde on Erspia-1. While a caricature of evil—no, not altogether a caricature, he and his followers committed real evil—Hoggora had treated Laedo hospitably, intrigued to have such an exotic visitor. Laedo was hoping he would fare similarly among the gnomes, if they didn't try to seize his spaceship.

It would, of course, be a great advantage to have someone along who could introduce him. Laedo was really here to see if a rescue attempt was practicable. On the way in he had looked for a nearby clearing where he could put the spaceship down. There was one a mile or so away. Then there was the question of guards. If the prisoners were heavily guarded, he would have to abandon the idea.

It didn't seem that they were. The fairies had only a loose social structure and disliked routine. After all, if the gnomes managed to break their cages and escape, they would simply be captured again. There was nowhere for them to go.

"Would you like us to escort you back to your flying house?" Flit enquired politely.

"Just back to where we entered the forest, thanks."

He took careful note of his surroundings as they walked beside the stream. He recalled how Histrina had described the childlike innocents of Erspia-2 as 'like fairies'. Perhaps there was something to that. The winged people of Erspia-3 were far too trusting.

None of the tree villages which usually were scattered about the forest seemed to be anywhere nearby. The prisoners were placed from distance from any habitation. Which, too, was convenient.

Abducting the gnome would undoubtedly sour his relations with the fairies. They had accepted his tale of coming from some unknown world, and seemed content to leave him and Histrina to their own devices. But before long he would be questioned as to his future intentions.

He and Flit soared up through the vent in the forest and went separate ways, Laedo back to the projector station. He wanted to check out his cargo carrier before nightfall.

It was not very often that he saw flying folk over the forest canopy. The population of Fairyland was not large, and the fairies did not spend their time flitting about in the upper air. Their economy was simple. They gathered fruit, nuts and vegetables from their copious environment, and seemed never to have heard of agriculture.

There was one occasion when they did soar far above the forest. That was when courting or lovemaking. Flight seemed to be inextricably linked with sex. Couples would hurtle, swoop and pirouette, then mate on the wing, membranes thrumming.

Laedo thought he saw some such display as he approached the projector station, but he received a surprise on coming closer. Not two, but several figures were involved. And one of them was Histrina.

She had shown her usual enterprise during his short absence. She had found the spare gravpack and had learned how to use it. Now she was disporting in the air with three female fairies, laughing wildly.

The fairies clearly found her playfulness infectious. They too were laughing, darting and dodging, as Histrina tried to catch them.

Then Histrina suddenly succeeded in seizing hold of one of them. Histrina's expression changed. She clamped her arms around the other girl's thorax, preventing her wings from beating, so that she was like a transfixed insect. Alarm came to the fairy's face as she realized she was helpless.

Histrina was looking evilly at the fairy girl's wings.

"Histrina!"

She looked round furtively on hearing Laedo's voice.

"Let her go!" Laedo ordered in a stentorian voice.

Histrina obeyed. The fairy girl fell a few feet, then fluttered away, glancing back before fleeing into the distance.

The others, too, were holding back, hovering, puzzled by events. Laedo pointed. "Back into the station, Histrina."

"You lied to me," Histrina accused as she adjusted the knob on the strap of her gravpack. "You said there wasn't another one of these."

"That was to keep you out of trouble."

Back in the station, he relieved her of the pack. "I like those fairies," she said. "The girls are so *delicate*." She leered. "Do you know what I'd like to do? I'd like to take one of them right up in the air, you know, really high, then break her wings and watch her go tumbling to the ground, trying to fly with broken wings. That would be fun, wouldn't it?"

"Histrina, you must behave yourself!" Laedo shouted. "Stop thinking those things! Do you know what these fairies will do to you if you do anything like that? They'll kill you!"

She pouted.

Laedo debated within himself. What to do with Histrina during his trip to Gnomeland? She was a danger to others and to herself if left alone. On the other hand, he would endanger her life if he took her to Gnomeland with him. Should things go wrong, the gnomes would kill him or take him prisoner.

All in all, her chances would be better in Fairyland than in Gnomeland. Unfortunately he could not put a time lock on the projector station and lock her in temporarily.

"I'm going on a trip tonight," he told her. "You are to stay here in the station, and not leave until I get back. Do you understand?"

"I suppose so."

Laedo decided that if he reached an understanding with the gnomes he would return and collect Histrina without waiting for the transductor to be manufactured.

Fairies did not care much for fire, and did not bother to light their homes after dark. As night fell the whole population would be asleep, though Laedo had been unable to ascertain whether a watch was kept on the world above. Probably not. He wouldn't put it past the fairies simply to assume that the gnomes would not attack by night.

With a final stern warning to Histrina, Laedo left the projector station and climbed up the hull to his cargo ship. Briefly he paused, looking overhead. Fairyland was very dark at night, due to there being little starlight, but the looming overhead landscape was not completely lightless. Glows and sparkles could be seen. The gnomes remained busy during the hours of darkness, tending their furnaces.

Once in his ship, he uncoupled it from the projector station. With a low whine the manoeuvring engine carried it through the darkness. Switching an external screen to infrared, he spotted the cleft in the canopy where he had planned to land. Softly, the cargo ship settled through the gargantuan trees and on to a moss-like surface.

Donning infrared goggles, he left the ship and set off. It was not long before he found the stream that led to the prisoner compound. In less than half an hour, he had arrived.

Cautiously he surveyed the enclosure through his goggles. Raucous snoring came from the cages. Incredibly, there were no guards at all. The domed clearing was empty of fairies. Presumably they relied on the strength of the cages to hold their captives.

Using a small flashlight, he sidled up to the nearest cage wherein slept the gnome he had talked with earlier. He directed the beam into the cage.

The creature was lying down, but was not asleep. The gnome had been waiting for him. Bulging eyes stared back over a rounded shoulder.

Laedo had a cutting tool in his pocket. Stealthily the gnome climbed to his feet and watched as the vibrating blade sliced easily through the thick timbers of the prisoner cage.

"Fairies could not do that," he whispered hoarsely, as if in appreciation.

"Do not wake the others," Laedo whispered back.

The bars fell away. The gnome stepped through and stood on the moss, looking about him and snuffing the air.

"Free," he whispered. *"Free."*

He looked again at Laedo. The ferocity in his eyes made Laedo wonder if he meant to kill his rescuer and free his own comrades. Laedo's hand went to the butt of his gun. But the gnome did not move.

Laedo gestured. "Follow me."

He kept the gnome in sight as they left the clearing and made their way along the bank of the stream by the dim flashlight. When they came to his cargo vessel he widening the flashlight beam and let the gnome see the humped shape. The gnome was clearly astonished. He stepped forward and ran his hand over the skin of the hull.

"How do you make such a big shape?" he said in his rasping voice.

"It would take a long time to explain. As I told you, I come from a world which is neither yours nor the fairies. A world a long, long way from here. I have no interest in your world, or in the fairies' world. I simply aim to return home."

The gnome took this in without comment, but with no sign of puzzlement. It was as if he digested the information and simply accepted it.

Laedo gestured the gnome to follow and mounted the steps to the port, opening it. With an air of mystification his new companion entered the cargo ship and padded down the short passage to the main cabin.

Arms akimbo, the gnome stood in the middle of the room, mouth open as he looked about him, eyes narrowed in concentration.

"You live here?"

"This is not a house," Laedo informed him. "It is a vehicle for travelling from place to place."

For the first time he inspected the single body-garment the gnome wore. It clung to his torso from shoulders to groin, and appeared to be made of greenish-coloured woven metal. Perhaps chain mail for protection against arrows, he thought.

He pointed to a couch. "Sit there. We're going up into the sky, to your own world."

He heard a gasp from the gnome as he switched on the external screen and the dark forest was revealed, dimly illumined by the ship's lights. The huge boles slid by as he lifted off using the manoeuvring engine. Then they were in the open air, stars shining through the ring-like gap between the two world-hemispheres.

At first the manoeuvring engine met little difficulty in raising the ship against Erspia's low gravity. Then, about a quarter of the way across the gap, the gravity field suddenly intensified. This answered another of Laedo's questions. The fairies had told him they were unable to fly to the upper world, even had they wanted to. He had assumed they did not have the stamina for such a long climb, but now he saw there was a different cause. The planetoid had two gravity levels. Up to a certain height gravity was slight, enabling the fairies to fly. Beyond that, a stronger field took hold, confining them to their world. It would also, he reflected, hem in the atmosphere — as well as prevent the fairies from launching themselves into space.

The engine groaned, but was able to cope with the increased gradient, just as it had on Erspias 1 and 2. Then, as it passed the midpoint, the ship suddenly appeared to be descending. Laedo flipped the vessel over so as to gain his bearings, bringing the other landscape below him.

He started nervously as the gnome left the couch and came to stand close by him. But the creature appeared to be offering no threat. He stared out of the screen at his homeland, glancing at the controls as Laedo manipulated them.

"What is your name?" Laedo asked, attempting a friendly tone.

"I am called Ruzzok."

"I am Laedo."

The gnome made no answer. Below them, the landscape of the 'upper' world loomed large. In infrared the fires proved dazzling and Laedo switched instead to image intensification. They viewed the land as if by daylight.

It was a ravaged world of smoke and fire, an industrial wasteland. Vast slagheaps spread far and wide, roads and tramways winding round them. No wonder the gnomes wanted the fairies' world: they had ruined this one. Probably, too, they were running short of ores and were having to reclaim metal from scrap.

True, there were stretches of greenery. The gnomes weren't stupid enough to end up with a deoxygenated atmosphere. But what woods and grasslands Laedo did see seemed to have grown on top of old slagheaps.

How deep did the gnomes burrow in their search for ores? Laedo could imagine them breaking through the exterior of their world-hemisphere, causing their entire atmosphere to go whistling into the void. Presumably the designer of Erspia-3 had incorporated some measure to prevent that happening.

"Where to, Ruzzok?"

The gnome grunted uncertainly, perhaps unable to recognise his homeland's geography from the air. Laedo sent the ship swinging over what looked like a line of blast furnaces. Nearby was an array of enigmatic shapes, and beyond that a level area composed of cinders or ash of some sort.

Gently he set the ship down on the cinders. As he neared the ground, gnomes turned to gape upward.

Laedo turned to his passenger. "All right, Ruzzok, I've kept my part of the bargain. I want you to do what you can for me in return."

Again Ruzzok grunted. Laedo led him down the corridor to the port, opened it, extended the steps, and invited him to take his leave. Already gnomes were running towards the ship from the direction of the industrial complex.

As he closed the port behind Ruzzok's back, Laedo wondered what had driven the gnomes to such manic metallurgical efforts. Surely they were not prompted by their economic needs, which must be simple. Perhaps it was obsessive behaviour, bred into them in accordance with their mythic characterisation.

He returned to the main cabin and watched events on the viewscreen. Ruzzok was talking to his compatriots and gesticulating up at the cargo carrier. Consternation and puzzlement appeared on a dozen gnome faces.

Let them keep guessing for a while, he told himself. He would sleep for a few hours, then see how his new hosts behaved.

When Laedo awoke the two suns had appeared and he was able to look out on his surroundings in broad daylight.

A group of gnomes squatted not far from his cargo ship, staring steadfastly up at it. All wore the same one-piece knitted metal garment worn by Ruzzok, but he was unable to tell if his short-time companion was present. They all looked alike to him.

Beyond the immediate area, which was covered in ash and clinker, were the tall shapes of furnaces and the big, strange contraptions he had seen earlier. His attention went to the latter. They sported immense long beams and massive laminated steel springs. At the end of each long beam was what looked like a cabin large enough to cram in four to six gnomes.

It was a minute or two before he guessed their purpose. These must be examples of the powerful catapults designed to propel cargoes high into the air and through the gravity barrier to the other world.

The machines were spectacular, both in appearance and in intention. Laedo wondered about the shock to the human body of being slammed into the sky in so sudden a manner. Presumably the tough, stocky gnomes were able to withstand it, but he wondered if all of them survived the experience.

Checking his handgun for charge, he opened the port, extended the steps, and stood in the doorway looking out. At the first threatening move, he had decided, he would retreat into the ship and take off.

At his appearance two of the gnomes rose to their feet and walked forward. As they mounted the steps one of them gave him a nod and a look of recognition. It was Ruzzok.

He led them into the main cabin and invited them to be seated. They ignored this and continued to remain standing, their bearing stiff.

Ruzzok spoke. "This is Mezzen, mechanic and engineer. Tell him what it is you want."

Briefly Laedo studied the newcomer. He had the same stolid impassivity as Ruzzok himself. It was impossible to read anything from his face.

"What metals do you work in, here in Gnomeland?" he asked.

The answer was fiercely proud. "We work in steel!"

Laedo nodded. He rummaged in a drawer and came out with the sketch he had made for Hoggora's metal-worker, spreading it in front of the gnome technician.

"Can you make this? It has to be exact to the specified measurements, to one part in a thousand."

One part in a thousand was barely enough in fact, but Hoggora's man had been incapable of achieving anything like that. Laedo imagined that it would push the gnomes' ideas of precision engineering to their utmost as well.

Mezzen peered at the drawing for a while.

"We can make it," he pronounced.

"How long will it take?"

The gnome shrugged, and looked about him. "How long did it take your people to make this vehicle?"

Laedo gave an embarrassed laugh. "I've no idea."

"Why do you want this part made?"

Laedo saw no reason to lie. "So that I can return home to my own world far off in space. My ship is damaged and I am stranded here."

"Then this is a matter of great importance to you," the gnome replied quickly. "If we are to help you, you must help us."

"I have helped you already. I rescued Ruzzok."

Mezzen pulled a face, increasing his ugliness to a quite extraordinary degree. "What of his comrades who are still prisoners of the fairies? You did not rescue those."

The meeting was not going as Laedo had hoped. "I took a risk in rescuing even Ruzzok. If I had tried to release the others the fairies would have been upon us."

Grunting his scepticism, Mezzen then said, "How many of us gnomes do you think this vessel could carry? Fifty? A hundred? Damaged though I assume it is, since it cannot take you home, it still brought you here from the world of the fairies. So it can return there as well. You could travel to and fro, transporting large numbers of us to assist the coming invasion."

Mezzen looked at him steadily as he added, "Be our friend and we will be yours."

Laedo reminded himself that all previous invasions had failed. In all likelihood this was because the gnomes' catapults could not fling enough troops and materials to the other half of the split worldlet.

Ethically, he could not for one moment consider siding with the gnomes in their grotesque ambition. It looked like he would have to return to Fairyland and get to work on the projector station's command system.

A thought occurred to him. Erspia-3 was similar to Erspia-1 in some ways. On the latter, the planetoid had also been divided, by 'good' followers of Ormazd and 'bad' followers of Ahriman. The dichotomy was more complete on Erspia-3, with two landscapes facing one another across a ten mile gap. On the one were the peaceful, delightful fairies. On the other, the belligerent, rapacious gnomes.

Perhaps the legendary Klystar liked to play with the good and evil aspects of the human psyche, separating them and allowing them to struggle with one another in various ways.

Another thought struck him. The surface gravity on Gnomeland was as weak as on Fairyland, but there appeared to be no need for it, since the gnomes did not fly. Why . . . ?

Of course. It was to enable the gnomes to reach Fairyland so as to engage in warfare with its inhabitants. Everything had been planned from the start, just like placing a bridge between two formicariums so as to watch the two nests of ants fight one another.

Including the improbability that the gnomes could actually succeed in conquering Fairyland using their own resources. Laedo's cargo ship could tip the balance in their favour.

"I shall have to think about it," he said.

"What is there to think about?" Mezzen challenged, his voice loud and suspicious. "Our interests converge. You wish to have your ship repaired. We wish to take possession of the land in the sky. We can give each other what we want."

His voice fell. "Or are you really here as a spy for the fairies?" he rumbled. "To report on our preparations?"

"I do not wish to see anything of your preparations," Laedo replied mildly. "There is no reason why I should act for the fairies. They cannot manufacture a steel part for me."

He stepped towards the portal. "Please give me a few hours to think about this. I will come out and speak to you when I have decided."

Silently Mezzen and Ruzzok followed him along the corridor. Laedo opened the port.

"Hold him," Mezzen snapped.

Two more gnomes were standing on the platform at the top of the steps. They pointed weapons at Laedo's chest.

These were not the long spears or elegant longbows favoured by the fairies. They were compact, powerful-looking crossbows, lever-drawn, trigger-operated. In the groove of each cross-piece rested a wicked steel bolt. Paralysis seized Laedo as he saw the gnomes' forefingers curled tensely around those triggers. He felt unable either to reach for his gun or to press the stud which would close the port. Instead he raised his hands and backed away, almost bumping into the two coming up behind him.

"We will keep our bargain once the war is over," Ruzzok promised him. "We will help repair your ship."

They took him back to the main cabin. "Now," Mezzen said, "show us how to work this vehicle."

"You won't be able to do it," Laedo claimed. "It takes years of training."

In fact he imagined the gnomes would be able to master the controls quite quickly once they had been demonstrated, at least as far as the close manoeuvring engine went. That was all they would need to fly between the two landscapes.

"That may or may not be true," Mezzen replied thoughtfully. "If it is, you can fly the machine for us."

Laedo realized he was being threatened. Did he face torture? He was beginning to curse his rashness in coming here.

"What if I simply take it up in the air then crash it, killing everyone on board?"

"You would die too."

"I do not like being forced to do something."

Mezzen, with what Laedo thought was uncanny perspicuity, approached the control board. His eyes darted quickly about the slides and keys. Suddenly he turned to the others.

"Take him away. We will experiment."

As he was hustled through the door, down the steps and across the ash-covered ground, Laedo took comfort in the fact, incredible though it seemed at first, that the gnomes had not relieved him of his handgun. The reason was obvious once he thought of it. The object was not a weapon in their eyes. It was simply an ovoid shape, moulded to provide a handgrip.

Now, he thought, should be the time to use it. But the prospect of one of those metal bolts tearing through his body stayed him. Besides, he did not know if he would have the stomach to kill the number of gnomes necessary to make his escape.

Perhaps under cover of darkness he could slip away from wherever he was to be held and recover the ship . . . Such vague thoughts in his mind, a bolt-laden crosspiece still nudging his back, Laedo was marched beneath the huge catapult machines which he now saw closely for the first time. The beams on which the small cabins were perched were angled high in the air. Whole batteries of windlasses worked winding mechanisms for forcing down those arms, ready to be released with bone-shattering force.

Now they passed a line of blast furnaces and searing heat scorched Laedo's skin. The gnomes tending the furnaces seemed able to work incredibly close to their roaring mouths, as though they were impervious to heat. Further off could be seen a complex of metal-roofed sheds, probably factories and work-shops.

A great mound of tailings loomed ahead. Laedo was con-ducted round it and saw, some distance away, the entrance to a downsloping tunnel. The gnomes urged him towards it, and soon he was being taken underground.

The walls of the tunnel were rough-cut rock, the roof but-tressed with timber supports. Flickering light came from sput-tering lamps set in cressets. At intervals side tunnels appeared, into which or out of which gnomes passed, carrying digging tools: pickaxes, shovels and rakes.

Was iron ore or coal mined here? Laedo presumed Klystar had stocked the planetoid with both, otherwise the gnomes would quickly have denuded their world of its forests in their need for charcoal for smelting.

His question was answered when a wagon went past them hauled by a team of four sweating gnomes. It was piled high with what he presumed to be ore.

At length he was pushed roughly into a side tunnel. A gnome of unusually large size confronted them, fangs reaching up half his face, a whip dangling in one hand.

One of the two who had brought him here spoke. "This is a prisoner, not a slave. He is not to be put to work unless other-wise ordered."

The big gnome trailed the lash of his whip negligently on the dust-strewn floor of the tunnel. "He can be quartered with the others just the same."

The others left, clearly assuming that the big fellow could handle Laedo if need be, even though armed with nothing but his whip.

Still Laedo did not resort to his gun. This was the first he had heard that the gnomes used slaves, and he was curious. The overseer, if that was what he was, cracked the whip and in-clined his head on its bull-like neck, indicating that Laedo should proceed down the side tunnel ahead of him. Laedo obeyed. About fifty yards along an opening led into a bulbous chamber.

It was a slave sleeping quarters. When Laedo saw the 'slaves' he received a surprise. Four naked, begrimed fairies lay on the floor, looking up with sleepy woe as he and the gnome entered. They seemed to shrink instinctively away from the whip which the overseer trawled absent-mindedly to and fro in the dust.

Yes, they were fairies, but something was wrong. Twin stumps jutted from their backs.

Their wings had been cut off.

"Stay here until you're sent for. Don't wander off. Food will be brought to you."

The overseer left. Laedo stared at his fellow prisoners, who stared back with little sign of interest. Two were male, two female, and their backs were scarred from whipping.

"How long have you been in Gnomeland?" he asked.

After a pause, one of the males answered in a listless murmur.

"We were born here."

"There are others? Fairy folk, I mean?"

"A few."

The gnomes must have contrived to bring back prisoners during one of their earlier excursions to Fairyland, Laedo reasoned. These were their descendants.

The slight, light-boned fairies would hardly make ideal slaves. Physically they were puny compared with the gnomes. Probably they were used in a spirit of triumph and domination — a grim foretaste of what would transpire should the gnomes gain possession of the other world. As it was, it looked as though these four were being worked to death.

The slaves sank back into their exhausted sleep. Laedo sat with his back to the chamber wall. He glanced at his timepiece. It would be dark in ten hours.

Thoughts of karma assailed him. If the gnomes succeeded in learning to control his cargo ship and as a consequence conquered Fairyland, it would be as a result of his ill-considered actions. Bad karma indeed.

After a while the overseer returned and kicked the fairies awake. It was time for their shift. They dragged themselves to their feet and staggered out, clinging to the walls for support. Never, Laedo reflected, had they known the pleasure of soaring through the air, of passing through leafy glades or settling on giant boughs with the poise of butterflies. He considered what he might do about it. On Fairyland, crippled though they were, they would be looked after—or so he assumed, provided the fairies did not have some unsuspected hard attitude towards deformity.

Another de-winged girl fairy entered, also naked. She thrust a bowl of slops at him, leaving without meeting his eye.

Raising the greenish mess to his nostrils, Laedo laid it aside after sampling its vile aroma.

There was nothing to do but wait. He laid his head against the rock and tried to doze, ignoring the comings and goings in the tunnel outside the chamber.

Eventually he was roused by the return of the four fairies whose sleeping chamber this was. They scarcely seemed able to stand, flinging themselves to the floor as soon as they entered.

They were unwilling to answer questions, but Laedo persisted. "Have you ever thought of escaping?" he asked.

"Escaping to where?" one of the fairies replied wearily. "The gnomes are everywhere."

"What if you could go to Fairyland, where there are no gnomes, only people like yourselves?"

"Is there such a place? It is only a fable our parents liked to tell."

They all closed their eyes and soon were snoring. Laedo waited a little longer. He noticed that there was less activity in the tunnel lately. It seemed the gnomes scaled down their work at night.

He shook the fairies awake, ignoring their fatigue. "There really is a fairy world," he said. "I can take you there. Come with me."

"You are a fool," said the male who had spoken earlier. He looked at Laedo in puzzlement. "You cannot defy the gnomes."

"Watch this," Laedo said. He unhitched his gun from its holster, adjusted the setting, and directed a beam at the side of the chamber.

They stared in disbelief as melted rock trickled down the wall.

"See? This is a better weapon than the gnomes have. And I know a way to get to Fairyland."

One of the females shook her head hysterically. "No! We must stay here! The gnomes will kill us if we try to leave!"

Her reasoning was probably correct. Laedo's plan, simple as it was, had every chance of going wrong. But in his view the chance was worth taking, and it was the only chance they would ever have. So he was making the decision for them.

"If you insist on staying here, *I* will kill you," he promised.

That seemed to frighten them into compliance. They had probably seen slaves killed for disobedience.

The only light the chamber had came from the nearest cresset in the tunnel. Laedo edged himself through the entrance, peering this way and that and listening intently.

No gnomes were in sight. And there was no sound of movement, not even the distant chinking of pickaxes he had earlier heard echoing through the tunnels.

"Come with me."

"But it is our time to sleep!"

"Sleep later." Laedo waved his gun. *"Come with me!"*

They obeyed. Proceeding down the tunnel, Laedo found he could extinguish the cressets by throwing a handful of dust on them. He created darkness behind them as they went. They turned into the main tunnel, which was also deserted, and sidled close to one wall until gaining the surface.

As on Fairyland, the structure of the split world, with its moonless, almost starless night, was an advantage. Overhead loomed the blank darkness of the opposite landscape, unenlivened by the light of fires. Only a few stars glinted through the gap between the two horizons, forming an embracing ring of distant points.

Otherwise the night was relieved by uneven glares from the blast furnaces. Laedo realized that he and the fairies would have good cover from the sight of any gnomes tending those furnaces, if they made their way round the other side of the big mound of tailings which separated the mine entrance from the open space where his ship was parked—if the ship was still there and had not been flown away by the determined Mezzen. The wingless fairies huddled with fright and unfamiliar cold as they came into the open. He herded them forward, anxious to get into the mound's shadow.

Blackness engulfed them as the furnaces disappeared behind the bulk of the pile. The fairies moaned in bewilderment as they stumbled in complete darkness, until Laedo took the risk of bringing out his flashlight, tuning it to a diffuse, dull glimmer.

Treading crushed ore, they crept round the mound until emerging on its further side. Laedo smiled as, by the faint light washing across from the furnaces and filtering through the angular shapes of the catapult machines, he saw his cargo ship.

It lay on its side. Mezzen's efforts had been rewarded with some success, evidently, but not enough. He had managed to turn on the manoeuvring engine, but had been unable to control it.

Laedo wished he could have witnessed the looks on the faces of the gnomes as their 'experimenting' caused the cargo ship to tilt over and crunch on to the cinders, creating chaos in the lounge/control room. Presumably the problem had been left to await the dawning of the next day.

He turned to whisper to the fairies, pointing to the ship. "See that? That's what we're headed for. Quickly now, follow me."

He went loping across open ground, not too fast in case the weary fairies were too weak to keep up with him. He paused before the looming ship, brought out his remote and ordered the steps to descend.

The steps emerged from the foot of the now horizontal doorway, sensed that the ground lay in the wrong direction, and skewed themselves round in order to reach it. Laedo dashed up the crazy staircase and opened the port, then turned and gestured, calling out in a low voice.

"Up the stair, quickly! I'm taking you to Fairyland!"

They hesitated at first, then one of the females bravely took the lead, clambering up the steps. Encouraged by her example, a male followed. As she reached him, Laedo shoved her through the port and told her to keep going.

"Halt! Stand where you are!"

The voice was vibrant and raucous, a gnome voice. Gnomes were running across the open ground, taking aim with crossbows.

"Hurry!" Laedo shouted. He began to panic as he pushed the second fairy through the port. In the low gravity the gnomes were bounding across the cinders with phenomenal speed, like bouncing balls. At the foot of the stairs, the remaining male fairy gallantly urged his companion to ascend.

With alacrity she did so. Halfway up, a crossbow bolt took her full in the back. She tumbled from the steps with a dying gasp. Laedo glimpsed the tip of the bolt protruding from her chest.

He pulled his gun from its holster once more, and steeled himself to an act of violence.

He fired at one of the advancing gnomes. He had scarcely ever used the gun before, and his aim was bad. The beam missed. He kept it on continuous and sent the beam wavering around until it found its target. The gnome's legs collapsed under him as his life was extinguished.

Laedo was screaming furiously to the remaining fairy, who instead of racing up the stair was examining the female to see if any life remained. He had left it too late. Two bolts hit him at once, one in the head, the other through the ribs.

A gnome appeared at the foot of the stairs, snarling up at Laedo. He had already discharged his crossbow and had no time to reload. He threw it away, trod carelessly on the male fairy, and scrambled upward, reaching for Laedo.

Hurriedly Laedo pointed the emitter of his gun and pressed the stud. The big, ugly face melted and charred. The gnome fell to join the two fairies in death.

Backing at a crouch through the doorway, Laedo thankfully closed the port. It was awkward making his way along a corridor that lay on its side, but at least he was safe now. He grinned as he heard crossbow bolts raining against the hull with banging, clattering sounds. They would make little impact against a hull built to withstand space debris travelling at high speed.

He wondered whether he should feel bad. Two of the fairies had met their deaths because of him.

No, he decided, he should not feel bad. He had estimated the risks and made a calculated decision. Given time to think, the fairies themselves might regard death while attempting to escape better than a life of misery and servitude.

The two who had survived were in the lounge, squatting in consternation on the wall which now served as a floor. Contriving to gain the control board, he set the ship gravity to a low level and switched it on.

With squeals of alarm, the fairies slid to the real floor and clung to one another.

Laedo switched on the close manoeuvring engine, raised the ship off the ground and brought it upright. He switched on the external screens and turned them to image intensification so as to be able to see clearly by what little light there was.

The cargo carrier soared idly over the scene below. Gnomes were swarming like ants. Then Laedo observed to what purpose. One of the catapult machines was being frantically cranked. At the same time it was being rotated, on some sort of turntable. It could be aimed.

The cabin was removed. In place of it came a simple bowl, and into this a large rock was being levered with great effort.

Laedo took the ship higher. Seconds later, the catapult flung aloft its projectile.

The rock came surprisingly close, passing within yards. Laedo watched as it continued upward until it dwindled into invisibility. Was it destined to crash somewhere in Fairyland's forests?

Now more engines were being wound down. Laedo doubted that the missiles could knock his ship out of the sky even if one struck, but he didn't want to take the chance. He headed for the world overhead.

On the way, he reflected that on Erspia-1 he would not have found matters as easy as he had on both Fairyland and Gnomeland. In some ways the fairies and the gnomes remained simpletons. They were too separated to have learned astuteness through regular contact with one another.

Was Klystar or his agents observing their behaviour? Were there watching devices recording all that took place? Laedo still had no better explanation for this group of worldlets than the one given by the staff of the Ormazdian projector station. Klystar was studying human nature.

He turned to the two fairies he had succeeded in rescuing.

"It's all right," he reassured them. "You're going to a better world. Sleep now, if you want."

They stared at him, stunned at the sudden change in their circumstances, but they asked no questions. It was as if their ingrained habit of obedience was now transferred to him, for they lay down on the floor, closed their eyes, and soon were asleep.

Briefly he felt the ship go through the inertial barrier, then he turned it round to descend on the other landscape. Again using the image intensifier, he cruised around until he located the clearing where the projector station was parked, and settled down beside it.

Then he, too, decided to sleep, and retired to his rest cubicle.

He had set the timer to wake him an hour after daylight. Returning to the lounge, he found the fairies still asleep. In all probability they had little or no knowledge of day and night. They woke and slept at the behest of the gnomes.

After a leisurely breakfast he went outside. Best to check if Histrina had behaved herself, he thought.

He found no sign of her in the projector station. Re-emerging, he scanned the sky.

Up above, he saw what looked like a pair of strange birds writhing together far aloft, as though in a mating dance, or else fighting. Suddenly they plummeted, then just as abruptly, checked their fall.

Laedo ran back into his ship, switched on an external viewscreen and directed it upward at full magnification. What he saw made him hold his breath, cursing his oversight in not taking the gravpacks with him on his sojourn to Gnomeland, instead of carelessly leaving them in the projector station.

Histrina was wearing one of the gravpacks and was once again disporting with some fairy girl, expressly against Laedo's orders. She was laughing, her features ugly with sadistic glee. The fairy was clutching at her, panic on her face.

Histrina had broken both her wings, which twitched and trailed uselessly.

With a cry Laedo ran from the ship and into the projector station. He quickly found the second gravpack, strapped it on, dashed outside and surged into the air.

So engrossed was Histrina in what she was doing that she failed to see Laedo coming. She tore the fairy girl's grip free of her clothing and held her up by her forearms, staring avidly into her terrified, helpless face. Then, despite the injured girl's pleas, she dropped her.

With a wail the fairy plummeted slowly past Laedo, steadily accelerating in the low gravity and instinctively trying to scull the air with her broken wings, which fluttered pathetically behind her. Laedo's hand went briefly to his gravpack's control knob. He swooped after her, caught her deftly in his arms and felt her cool, slim arms go desperately round his neck.

He headed away from the station towards where he knew there was a tree village. His hope was that the fairies had medical skill and would know how to mend the girl's broken wings. If not, he would offer to attempt help with his ship's facilities.

Dipping into the lush and pleasant foliage, he dropped into a flower-bedecked bower and flew along it until coming in sight of a flat expanse which was actually a fork between two gargantuan boughs. It was like coming upon the central green of an ancient village, for clustered around it at various levels were picturesque tree houses, perched cottages roofed with giant leaves. Laedo alighted on the moss-covered bark.

Emerging from doorways, fairies glided or stepped to where Laedo gently laid his burden on the moss, careful of her bedraggled wings. He turned to the villagers, seeing their dismay.

"She has been injured," he said. "If you cannot mend her, bring her to me."

With that he was off again, back to the projector station and Histrina. He found her lying on her back on the grass, limbs outspread, eyes closed in a posture of utter contentment.

The gravpack lay beside her. Laedo snatched it up, at which Histrina opened her eyes and sprang to her feet.

"Oh, that was *go-o-o-od,*" she growled softly. Then she suddenly became angry and accusing. "But you spoiled it! You caught her!"

Arching her fingers like a cat, she struck out to scratch his face. The gravpack dangling by its straps from one hand, he fended her off with the other and slapped her hard.

"What did I tell you?" he bellowed. "And what do you expect the fairies to do about this?"

She nursed her reddened cheek. "They can't do anything. They've only got bows and arrows and spears. We've got your gun."

"I've got my gun." He snatched it from its holster and pointed the beamer at her. "Maybe I should use it on you. Now

get back in the station and stay there."

Sullenly she obeyed, glancing back at him with resentment. Laedo waited until she had disappeared into the station, then went into the cargo ship.

The wingless fairies came sleepily awake as he entered, looking at him half from curiosity, half from fear. He fed them, then took them outside to gawp at the scenery.

"This is the world where you belong," he told them. "This is what the gnomes took your ancestors away from and made them slaves. Here there are other fairies like yourselves who will help you. There's just one thing wrong."

He paused. "The other fairies have wings and can fly in the air. The gnomes cut yours off when you were young. Do you know that?"

They nodded. The male replied. "The story is passed down that what the gnomes remove is for flying. But we never really believed it. It's just that they would get in the way when working in the tunnels."

"It's true. Here, fairies fly. Unfortunately your wings cannot be restored to you. But with these devices on your backs you can still fly, as if you had wings." He indicated the gravpacks. "Then you can take your proper place here."

He had feared that the two would be too crushed by their life experiences to be able to learn anything new. He was proved wrong. They had, after all, been raised in an atmosphere of engineering, and the gravpacks were simple to use.

His second fear, that they would be frightened and bewildered by height, was also wrong. Their instinct to fly asserted itself almost immediately. He started with the man fairy, taking him into the air and showing how to use the single control, then he showed the girl. In less than an hour they had both mastered the whole thing.

Back on the ground, he solemnly made presents of the packs. "Go in that direction," he said, pointing. "Keep looking until you find people like yourselves. Explain your story to them and they will help you."

They took to the air, circling one another and laughing with incredulous delight. Then they set off, low over the forest canopy.

Now there was nothing to do but wait.

The five-men commission came late in the day, spiralling down into the clearing to settle themselves cross-legged on the grass, where they confronted Laedo grim-faced.

Among them Laedo recognised Highbreeze, the air marshal he had met on the day of his arrival. But he was not at the head of the commission. This was a somewhat elderly figure announcing himself as Wafting Leaf. "The young woman whom your companion crippled has received the attentions of the healers," he said, "but it will be a hundred days before she can take to the air again, if she ever does."

He raised his eyes to the cargo ship and projector station before continuing. "By our laws your companion's act is punishable by death. Also, we deduce that it was you who released the gnome prisoner and that you took him back to Gnomeland. This also is punishable by death. Against these crimes we are obliged to balance the fact that you saved the crippled young woman Red Petal's life, and that you rescued two mutilated fairies from Gnomeland. We have questioned these two. There are legends that gnomes kidnapped babies long ago, but frankly we are shocked to learn that members of our race are kept by them as slaves, and in such horrible conditions.

"Before pronouncing judgment, I must ask why you went to Gnomeland in the first place."

Laedo decided to tell something close to the truth.

"My only aim is to return home," he said. "I had hoped the gnomes would help me repair my ship, and I took the prisoner with me to try to earn their good will. Instead they took me prisoner. Luckily I managed to escape."

Wafting Leaf nodded and appeared to accept the account. "I can only observe that you badly misjudged the gnome character. Such ignorance supports your claim to belong to neither of our worlds. We now come to judgment. In your case, one act cancels out the other. But not in the case of your companion. There is still the matter of poor Red Petal's broken wings."

"I can only apologise for my companion," Laedo said. "She suffers from a mental illness. This causes her to act badly. I hope to have her condition treated by experts when I return to my own world."

Wafting Leaf considered this. "If what you say is true, you should not have left her at liberty."

Laedo lowered his gaze and was silent, recognising the truth of the other's words.

Wafting Leaf spoke again. Laedo had been nervous that the fairies would ask him to enable an attack on Gnomeland, in an effort to rescue every slave there — an enterprise for which he felt more sympathy than the project proposed by the gnomes, but for which he had zero willingness, particularly in view of its impracticability. The elderly fairy's pronouncement, therefore, came as a relief.

"It seems best that you should leave our land as soon as possible. We will defer the death sentence upon your companion for ten days, in recognition of your need to effect repairs. Meanwhile, you are forbidden to have any further contact with our people."

With grave dignity the five fairies rose and launched themselves aloft to go winging into the distance.

Laedo sighed. Ten days. He reminded himself that he still had little or no idea of how he was to gain control of the station's command system.

The only warning was a steely glinting of metal in the early morning sky. It was as if the flat upside down landscape had begun to sparkle and glitter.

Then the glints blossomed into tiny white flowers which grew as they descended. Soon gnome-crammed cabins were landing all over Fairyland.

And not just cabins. Batches, packets and tied-together bundles of materials floated down under the big parachutes, even components of the big catapult machines ready to assemble for communication back with Gnomeland.

It was the biggest gnome invasion Fairyland had yet seen.

One which Laedo, as he watched the wicked snowfall, was forced to recognize had probably been precipitated by himself. The gnomes, concerned that he would warn the fairies of their plans, had struck ahead of schedule.

One question was answered for him. The gnomes *did* have telescopes. They knew where he was. A cluster of cabins was targeting the clearing. As they came nearer he saw guide cords tugging at the edges of the parachutes, giving a measure of guidance.

It was only one day after the commission's judgment. So far all Laedo had done was to affix his cargo ship atop the projector station as before, and remove some panels under the main board in the control room, hoping he could figure out some way to bypass the automatic control. He had just woken up after a night's sleep and come outside for some fresh air.

A long shadow fell across him. A billowing parachute was sailing over the giant treetops and heading towards him.

A crossbow bolt hissed aslant and bit the turf near his foot.

Laedo yelped and ran for the projector station's stair. He made it inside and sealed the hull as the first cabin was tumbling to the ground.

In the control room, he switched on the screens and yelled at the control board.

"Klystar is not here! We are under attack! Take us to Klystar!"

This time no parchment chattered out of the slot. The station shuddered slightly and lifted itself. Crossbow bolts clanged on the outside hull. The station topped the forest canopy and soared majestically into the air.

Already the fairy militia had risen to meet the attack. He saw fairies winging about the descending cabins, exchanging shots with the cramped passengers. Some were armed with long pikes with which they tried to sever the parachute lines — a manoeuvre which usually was usually rewarded with a crossbow bolt through the chest.

Laedo saw one brave fairy charge in to jab between the bars of a cabin with a spear, only to become tangled in the parachute cords. The parachute collapsed and candled. Fairy and gnomes fell together to their deaths.

Still ascending, the station passed through a second wave of cabins, parachutes not yet released. Then it was heading for the gap between the two opposed horizons.

Where to now?

FIVE

A Map of Moods

The railway line wound through the broken landscape, curling round hills, clinging to escarpments and diving into valleys. The train of little box-shaped carriages climbed a steep incline by means of cogwheel and ratchet, then went rattling down the other side, swaying alarmingly on the narrow-gauge track.

To the relief of the passengers it adopted a more moderate speed on coming to a levelled embankment, its burnished engine puffing and chuffing. Munching a meagre meal of crispbread spread with fish-flavoured soft cheese, Adeptus Magus Harmasch and his apprentice Peadul stared glumly out of the window.

"Eh, Peadul, what a place," Harmasch sighed. There was nothing to be seen but an oppressive grey sky, rocky crags and boggy ground pelted with cold, penetrating rain.

Thus was it ever in the country of Brodonia. The rain never stopped. The sun never shone. And the people were forever miserable.

Magic did not work here, either.

"I feel so unhappy I could kill myself," apprentice Peadul complained. "Why do the Brodonians continue living? Or at least why don't they move elsewhere?"

Despite his gloom Harmasch chuckled. "The people here like their misery," he explained. "It is their mental climate, and if they travel abroad they always want to return to it, just as we want to return to the merriment of Cherie, our own country. Still, it is good to travel and experience foreign emotions."

"Well, I still feel like killing myself."

"To be honest, I also will be glad when we reach the border."

The train continued to trundle on its way, swaying through fog and rain. Occasionally it stopped at some wretched halt around which clustered a few decrepit hovels, where pale faces streaming with rain peered in through the windows, as if the train's arrival was the only bright spot in their owners' wretched existence.

After what seemed like an interminable time the engine again ground to a standstill, hissing steam. They had reached the frontier. Before allowing the train to proceed, dour-faced border guards visited each carriage in turn, taking names and searching luggage.

Such was the routine. Anyone who entered Brodonia was recorded, anyone who left Brodonia was recorded, in case he had stolen something, or had committed some other crime, or was attempting to rescue a Brodonian from the country's weather.

At length the train chuffed slowly forward. For those on board it was like passing through a curtain. No transition could have been more sudden. The passengers entered bright sunshine and saw green meadows sprinkled with flowers, while the chill faded away behind them.

Looking back, the frontier could be seen as a wall of rain wavering its way from horizon to horizon. Harmasch chuckled as his mind emptied itself of despondency. Peadul, too, grinned with relief.

At first Harmasch's native chortling gaiety reasserted itself and he regaled Peadul with quips and jokes. Soon, however, the mood endemic to Pastorale, the country they had now entered, laid itself on him. This was a mood of tranquil delight in nature. The magician and his apprentice gazed delightedly at sunny meadows and neat green woods reeling past. What a change from miserable Brodonia!

Admittedly Brodonia was not the worst. Their journey had taken them through Feroce, a fiery land of roaring volcanoes and crashing lightning where the ruling emotion was one of angry exasperation. It had caused not a few of the train's passengers to come to blows.

The transit of Pastorale lasted less than an hour. Briefly they crossed a corner of Wymptia, a land of fatuous silliness where pink snow fell without pause even though the climate was warm and balmy.

The whimsical Wymptia mood passed the instant they crossed the frontier into Neutralia.

Neutralia: a small country, hardly more than a region, with no emotional climate of any kind. This was an eerie experience to come upon so abruptly, possibly one which only a trainee in magic could withstand. The train pulled into Klyston, Neutralia's single town, and ground to a halt at the central station.

Harmasch cleared his mind of distractions and aimed a thought at his apprentice.

Well, here we are, Peadul. Keep your wits about you.

Yes, master, Peadul thought back.

"Good, Peadul!" Harmasch congratulated out loud. "The atmosphere is marvellously clear here, is it not?"

And indeed it was. Magicians from all over Erspia were stepping down from the box carriages and on to the broad platform, making for a spacious plaza lying next to the station. All around them stood the white stone buildings of Klyston. The air was clear and bright, but somehow empty of quality, as though all mood colour had been extracted from it.

Perfect for the testing of magical ability.

After a shouted warning to any who had yet to embark or disembark, the train chuffed out of the station to continue its endless circling of the world.

The examinations were already in progress, some candidates having arrived by horseback or on foot. The place was familiar to Harmasch. He had been tested five times here, in order to reach his present grade of Magus Adeptus. He made his way with Peadul among the tables that had been laid out, and presented himself at the registration desk, displaying his certificate of wizardry with its five degrees.

"My apprentice here, Peadul Hobsot, applies for marking in the first degree."

Wearing a green shift, the registrar examined the certificate carefully. He scanned the plaza. "Place number seven is vacant. And please, Magus Adeptus, do not forget your cap."

"Of course," muttered Harmasch. He dipped into his bag and brought out his conical headdress with its five gold-coloured pentacles. He set it on his head.

Coloured balls were dancing in the air over the examination tables as they walked to table number seven. The examiner was a slim, middle-aged man who himself wore the cap of a Magus Adeptus. He smiled indulgently as Peadul settled himself nervously in the candidate's chair.

"This shouldn't take too long, young man."

Harmasch took the observer's chair a short distance away. In times past magicians had been known to cheat in favour of their apprentices, 'nudging' the results by using their own faculties. Any examiner worth his salt would soon detect such chicanery these days, but by convention a patron did not sit at the table.

"Now then," said the examiner affably, "I want you to recite the words I am thinking."

He closed his eyes, and Peadul did likewise. After a moment Peadul began to speak.

"The science of magic is the art of discipline of the mind. If the mind is not disciplined, magic cannot be performed. The magician learns to sustain a single thought for as much as an hour or more. He learns to extend his thoughts and mental images to the external world and to achieve effects through them."

Peadul paused, then spoke again in a different tone.

"Say, this is rather interesting."

The examiner opened his eyes and frowned. "Hmm. You seem to have picked up a stray thought from somewhere." He glanced in slightly reproachful fashion at Harmasch. This was a mark against Peadul: being unable to distinguish between one person's thought and another's.

"Let us move to the second test."

The examiner tipped a boxful of coloured balls into a curved hollow in the middle of the table. "Now. Let me see you perform the motions known as *Petals Dance in the Wind.*"

Peadul smiled. He had practised long on *Petals Dance in the Wind.* He fixed his eyes on the pile of balls, readied his mind, and reached out with his telekinetic faculty. The balls rose in the air and began gyrating in a complicated pattern, mauve following mauve, russet following russet, cobalt blue following cobalt blue, in winding streams. Intense effort of will was called for, each stream being moved independently but harmonising with the others. Smoothness of movement was required. The examiner would note any jerkiness or sudden drops indicating that the apprentice's telekinetic grasp had wavered.

Unfortunately just such dislocation occurred now. Kinks appeared in the gyrating streams. There was confusion in the dancing balls. Colours became mingled. With a gasp Peadul relinquished his power and let the balls cascade back into the recess.

He turned, not to the examiner, but to Harmasch. "Someone is interfering with my control!"

The two older men looked first at one another, then all around them. A little further off, standing between the tables, was a man who glanced furtively aside, as if trying to make himself invisible.

The person was of such odd appearance that it was surprising he had not been noticed before. He wore neither the conical cap of a magician nor the more common-place turban, but was bare-headed. His clothing was drab and without style: a single close-fitting blue overgarment, making it impossible to guess the mood of his native country. His features were unusual, too: sharp, with an angular nose and peculiar eyes.

To a Magus Adeptus the source of the sabotage was quickly evident. Harmasch and the examiner pointed, crying out together.

"Seize him!"

As the projector station flew over the landscape of Erspia-4, Laedo had seen spread below him what seemed to be a huge patchwork quilt. Slowly he realized that it was more like a map showing each country or political entity in a different colour. The colours resulted from the apparent fact that each country possessed its own unique weather, which ended sharply at clearly delineated borders. Sunny, stormy, tranquil, cloudy, fog-covered, and so on. The projector station came lower, and Laedo began to experience mood changes as he passed from one region to another. Delight, gloom, happiness, misery, fury, resignation, all flitted through his mind like wisps of cloud passing across the face of the sun. The transition from one emotion to another was as sudden and obvious as the edge of a moving shadow.

He suspected that he was in the presence of a social experiment similar to the one he had encountered on Erspia-1, but far more complicated.

Still outside his control, the projector station settled itself in a canyon in a bare, rocky region.

No sooner had it landed than a desire to kill Histrina

plopped full-blown into his consciousness. The impulse was sudden, vicious, and full of hatred.

He resisted the urge and walked out of the control room. He had not gone far when the murder mood vanished. Instead he was assailed by an almost overwhelming wish to commit suicide.

Moving experimentally from one part of the station to another, he was able to locate a borderline running through the structure. The station straddled a frontier. On one side was the impulse to murder, on the other, suicidal depression.

In both directions the area was bleak, rocky, lacking vegetation and without a population—though possibly it had possessed one once.

Laedo's experiences on Erspia-1 gave him the strength of mind to handle these unwelcome emotions. He treated them as originating from outside himself. This was not the case with Histrina. She made the most determined effort to murder him yet, and when he lured her into a part of the station on the other side of the invisible border, she had tried with equal enthusiasm to end her own life. His solution had been to drag her to his cargo ship and lock her in the lead cabinet which was, in effect, an isolation chamber proof against thought-rays. That was where she was now, with a store of air, food and water.

Laedo could hardly begin to guess what sort of control system could select both weather and emotions for demarcated regions on the planetoid. No orbiting projector stations showed up. Presumably everything was deep inside the worldlet, alongside the gravity generator.

Taking the cargo ship aloft for a brief reconnoitre, he had seen a town a few miles away. The murder and suicide areas were small, no more than localities. Evidently the projector station had chosen the canyon for concealment. Setting the cargo ship back in place, he had set out on foot, even though it occurred to him that Histrina would be in a poor situation should anything untoward happen to him.

On entering Neutralia he was pleased to find himself in a region free of artificially imposed mood. Wandering through Klyston, as he learned the town was called, he had come upon the grading examinations in magic.

Magic! It did not take him long to realize what this 'magic' consisted of. Klystar's technology had a finesse beyond anything he could have imagined. By some extraordinary technique of fine-tuning, thought projection was used to achieve telepathy between individuals. In similar manner, fine-tuned inertial fields projected from within Erspia-4 were made to respond to the human will and achieve telekinesis.

Not that the 'adepts' understood any of this. Neither did Laedo grasp what use these somewhat limited 'magical' powers were put to, nor why they were so valued on the planetoid. He did realize, however, that he had been rash indeed to experiment with the faculties himself, by interfering with the testing of a young apprentice. As a result he was accused of being a 'rogue wizard', mentally strong enough to exercise magic, but lacking the proper training. Such individuals were associated with Swirl, the land of continuous whirlwinds, whose people were eccentric mavericks and were forbidden to travel outside their borders because of their disordered lives. If they did, they were treated as outlaws.

He sat in a windowless room of white stone. Facing him across the table were the Magistrate of the Magical Convocation, the examiner whose work he had interrupted, and the magician whose apprentice he had wronged.

"Come now, admit it," said the magistrate testily. "You are a Swirlite who have unlawfully left your country. Tell the truth if you want mercy."

"I am not from Swirl, nor from any country on your world," Laedo answered ingenuously. He paused. "What do you call this world, by the way?"

"Erspia, of course! What else would we call it?"

"Yes, of course . . . but why do you call it Erspia?"

This time Harmasch spoke, in his usual jovial voice. "That is the name given to it by the creator, Klystar, and that is all that can be said about it."

"Klystar," said Laedo softly. "Did Klystar also teach you magic?"

"Naturally. Klystar made both the world and mankind, and gave us everything we have."

"And where is Klystar now?"

"Enough of this nonsense," the Magistrate retorted. "We already know that a band of Swirlites has broken out and is rampaging abroad, creating consternation to decent folk. It is quite clear to me that you are a member of that band. Where are your companions?"

"I know nothing of this country you call Swirl," Laedo insisted. "I do not even come from your world. I come from another world far off in space." He paused. "One that was not made by Klystar."

The examiner snorted. "Only a Swirlite could talk such arrant rubbish. Honoured Magistrate, I am anxious to resume the important task of testing, unmolested by this undisciplined individual. Could you not conclude the hearing in a satisfactory manner?"

"I am sorry for the way I intruded into your procedures," Laedo offered apologetically. "I can only say that I am ignorant of your customs and acted without considering the consequences. By the way, what is the penalty for such an offence?"

"It is death."

The Magistrate shifted in his seat. "For a Swirlite, at any rate. And since you have just admitted your guilt, it only remains for me to condemn you, with the comment that it is most unseemly for the annual testing to have to suffer such indignities. Take him to the execution ground."

"But wait a minute—"

Laedo had not expected this. He had even left his gun behind, assuming that the town he had seen in the distance would be peaceful. To bear weapons there might even be forbidden. But no one was prepared to listen to him. He was handcuffed, taken outside, bundled on to a horse-drawn cart, and this sent trundling over the flagstones.

The magician Harmasch, in his gold-starred, conical cap, clambered aboard as the cart began to move. Laedo's two guards glanced at him, but said nothing.

"Why do you say there are worlds not made by Klystar?" Harmasch asked. "That is a terrible blasphemy."

"Because it is true.," Laedo told him "Though Klystar did, for a fact, make a number of worlds. Do you know how many?"

"There is only one," Harnasch said reprovingly.

"No, there are more."

A small crowd of people began to follow the cart as it passed through the streets of the town. Their faces were passive but curious.

"Why is this town called Klyston?" Laedo asked.

"In honour of Klystar. It means 'Klystar's town'."

"Yes, of course," Laedo muttered. Then: "Where is Klystar now? Is there any way to reach him?"

"Whenever you perform magic, Klystar is reaching out to you. Otherwise you would be powerless. That is why it is wrong to meddle with these powers without the proper training and ceremonies, as you Swirlites do."

It was disappointing to meet with such superstition. Obviously the people of Erspia-4 had no real knowledge of Klystar.

Though there must have been some knowledge once. At least they knew his name.

And there was technical skill here. Laedo had seen a railway train coming through Klyston, pulled by a steam-powered locomotive. If things had not gone so badly wrong for him, perhaps he could have had his transductor made.

Or could he? A comical, almost ludicrous image came into his mind. Perhaps all machine parts were made by star-capped magicians in 'mentufactories', special places set aside by Klystar where thought-directed inertial fields could twist metal into pre-arranged shapes.

And why not? it seemed that nothing was too crazy for the Erspia worlds.

By now they were beyond Klyston and making for a bare moor. Laedo turned to the wizard.

"Listen to me. A few miles north of here is a large metal structure. A young woman is trapped in it. You must help her."

Harmasch did not even hear him. "Change your Swirlite heart in these your last moments. May you find peace in Klystar's bosom."

He dropped from the cart and began walking back to the town.

The cart stopped. Laedo was taken by the arms and helped to the ground.

A numbness of will had come over him. How did he arrive in this situation? How could he have behaved so incautiously in a new and unknown culture? The geniality and apparent harmlessness of Klyston's people had misled him, he told himself. He had been unable to imagine that they would put him to death for what was to him no more than a mischievous discourtesy.

Dire consequences were flowing from his failure. He was about to lose his life. Worse, he had incurred bad karma. He would never now be able to carry out his bound duty, which was to deliver his cargo of cavorite. And poor Histrina would die of thirst or suffocation, locked in the lead-lined cabinet.

The method of his execution was now revealed to him. A cord with a lead weight on each end was wrapped around his neck. The guards retreated, and as they did so the lead weights rose in the air.

A quartet of magicians surrounded him, keeping a distance of about twelve feet. They were concentrating, their eyes on the lead weights. The weights moved in diametrically opposite directions, tightening the cord, which bit into him.

He was being garrotted by 'magic'!

Choking, he fell to the ground, unable to raise his hands to stay the weights, which surged away from one another as if with a will of their own. There was a roaring in his ears. He felt his tongue being forced from his mouth.

Then suddenly, mercifully, the pressure eased. Magicians, guards and onlookers were fleeing with cries of alarm. He became aware of a chivvying call from the middle distance. *"Halloo! Halloo! Halloo!"*

He struggled to his knees, the strangling cord still uncomfortably tight about his neck. A troop of horsemen was rushing in at a gallop. They were a strange sight. Each rider held his steed's reins in his left hand and twirled his right arm over his head in a flailing motion. Each whirling arm seemed to be the base of an air vortex which caught dust and debris thrown up by the horses' hooves: a deliberately created dust devil. Furthermore the dozen or so vortices eventually joined up to form a minor whirlwind which accompanied the horesmen and trailed behind them.

These could only be 'Swirlites', practising their rogue magic upon the air, carrying a little piece of their whirlwind-ridden country with them as a flag or banner.

The whirlwind died as the riders reined in and jostled around Laedo. One dismounted and carefully unwrapped the ligature from around his neck. Then he drew a blade which was somewhere midway between a dagger and a broadsword, and with one deft slash severed the chain joining the handcuffs.

"Being nasty done to, oho? Not liking how you dingdong? Come swirl alongside."

With one leap the Swirlite was astride his horse. Reaching down, he pulled Laedo up behind him.

The troop cantered off the way it had come.

Laedo now had time to examine his rescuers. They were clad in makeshift garments, rags, or simply grass skirts. They seemed full of energy, chattering continually in clipped, disjointed phrases and ejaculations—a patois or slang which Laedo suspected they made up as they went along.

Most societies had their rebels who defied convention. It seemed the mood-mapped world of Erspia-4 had catered even for that.

Laedo wasn't much of a horseman, so he was glad when the Swirlites pulled up, dismounted and made camp. What followed was like an insane festival, a madcap round of capering, cavorting, yipping and hallooing, arms flailing over heads, air vortices bending this way and that, conjoining and separating.

The man whose horse he had shared, limbs bound about with bands, a brief cloth kilt hanging from his waist, his skin filmed with sweat from his exertions clapped an arm round Laedo and offered him a hunk of bread smeared with some foul-smelling cheese.

"You no straight, oho? No slave of Klystar's moods, oho? Like us, be you. Carry own craziness, oho? Bond with us to Swirl. Mad-happy."

Politely Laedo bit into the bread. No wonder these Swirlites were feared and hated. They were heretics. They rejected Klystar! Probably they failed to realize that their own mental outlook was not self-generated either. That, too, was dictated by Klystar's mood generators. An idiosyncratic state of mind was better able to maintain itself when crossing into other countries, that was all. Klystar had given Swirl all the advantages of lunacy.

Did the Swirlites have their own social outcasts, who lacked the vitality for a life of ceaseless partying and erratic behaviour? Laedo would certainly have been one of those. He ate the bread, then lay himself down a short distance away to get some sleep.

When he awoke it was dark and the Swirlites had finally tired themselves out. They lay sleeping, tumbled over one another, one or two draped over their horses. Laedo stole away by starlight and headed out in the direction he gauged the projector station lay.

It was not hard to find it. He knew when he had crossed the Neutralian border. Hot thoughts of killing entered his mind. He was in murder country. He found the canyon, then climbed up to his cargo ship.

What a relief it would be if he were to kill Histrina! No more keeping an eye on her, no more remorse for all the harm and killing *she* had done. No more having to think of her eventual welfare. Sometimes being ethical just didn't make any sense. He thought of what a pleasure it would be to choke the life out of her . . .

He forced the thoughts away and opened the cabinet. As he expected, she came at him with the strength of a madwoman, scratching, tearing and biting. Subduing her was difficult, but he did it by half-suffocating her. He dragged her into the projector station and tied her securely down to a couch, where she continued screeching her hatred once she recovered.

Wearily he spoke to the control board. "Take us to Klystar. Yet again."

Sedately the station rose into the star-speckled sky.

SIX

"Don't Love the Third One"

Before very long yet another Erspia worldlet glowed in the darkness, swelling until it almost filled the oval viewscreen. One could easily have imagined it to be a full-sized planet.

It displayed a new physical feature, though not one as bizarre as Erspia-3's. It possessed a moon.

The satellite was tiny, perhaps seven miles in diameter, and orbited just outside the shallow atmosphere. A natural body that size would have been irregular in shape, but this was no asteroid. It was spherical. Which meant that it had to be artificial, like its primary.

An equally artificial sun, occupying a wider orbit, lit both bodies. The projector station swooped towards the three-body formation, briefly fooling Laedo into thinking it was going to land on the moonlet. But then it veered aside and made for the planetoid.

Laedo glanced at Histrina. Since leaving Murder County (as he thought of it) she had calmed down, emboldening him to release her from her bonds. She had spent the first part of the journey describing the various gruesome ways to kill him that had occurred to her while down on the patchwork world, following that with an account of her past misdeeds, related in minute detail, together with thoughts of future sins she would like to commit. It was a dreary, insane litany, told in a maundering tone. Laedo was glad when she fell silent and watched the new world as it came closer.

The projector station deviated from the approach paths it had adopted earlier and circled Erspia-5 twice before entering the atmosphere. Gradually descending and losing velocity, it continued to hurtle above the landscape, allowing the character of the fifth Erspia world to become evident. It was a peaceful-looking planetoid of neat villages, ploughed fields and grazing herds. More than any of the others, it resembled Histrina's home world of Erspia-1, except that there were none of the swathes of destruction resulting from the conflict between

Ormazd and Ahriman.

The similarity possibly struck Histrina too. "People," she murmured, gazing on the villages as they passed by. "Lots of people. People to do things to."

"You're not going outside at all, unless you *swear* to behave yourself," Laedo countered firmly. "Even then I'll be watching you the whole time. One hint of trouble and I'll lock you up for the duration."

Histrina sank wearily on to the couch. "Oh, all right." She seemed not really interested. Maybe Murder County had burned her out. Either that, or being locked in the lead cabinet had brought her down.

Sailing low with all the majesty of a lighter-than-airship, the station seemed to be looking for a landing place. At length it settled on a grassy meadow just outside a medium-sized settlement.

The moon was a pale yellow orb in the sky, devoid of markings. There had to be a reason for its presence, Laedo thought. Was there intermittent war between it and the planetoid, as with the split world of Erspia-3?

Histrina spoke. "Let's not go outside yet. Let's fornicate first."

Laedo smiled faintly and shook his head. He couldn't be sure Histrina wouldn't use the occasion to bite through his jugular.

"Not tonight, Josephine."

"Josephine? Who's Josephine?"

"She was . . . well, never mind. I guess I'm no Napoleon, either."

"Napoleon? Who's Napoleon?"

Laedo ignored her. The viewscreen showed crop-bearing fields, as well as a pasture for sheep and another for cows. The outskirts of a village crowded the edge of the screen. The houses were picturesque: black timber beams and thatched roofs.

Men who had been working in the fields were looking up at the projector station with visible astonishment, but with a notable lack of alarm. The impression of imperturbability was reinforced when they came plodding calmly towards it.

Laedo wondered how many Erspias there were, each with its own artificially induced human quirk. Thousands? For that matter, how did they manage to hang together in a relatively small volume of space?

And was he doomed to tour them indefinitely in search of the mythical Klystar? Maybe he should stay inside and start ripping panels out to begin the possibly hopeless task of gaining control over the command system.

But in the end curiosity won out. Besides, there was always the hope of finding someone skilled enough to make a transductor for his cargo ship.

"We're going outside," he told Histrina. "Now remember, I meant what I said. I've had more than enough of your misbehaviour. If you kill anyone, or seriously injure anyone, *I'll* kill you. Myself. Straight away."

She looked startled, then pouted in her usual fashion. Most likely she didn't in the least believe him, and in that she was right. He saw her wickedness as an imposed evil, not her own fault. It would be unethical to kill her, unless absolutely essential in order to protect others.

But self-interest was the one thing she would understand and respond to, after all, and it might help to plant some small doubt in her mind.

"Well, let's go and see what's weird about those people out there," he said. "There's bound to be something."

Listlessly Histrina followed him to the portal. The stairway snaked down to the grass.

The three who had been approaching stopped to stare up at them with blank faces as they came out and stood on the platform. The clothing of the villagers was typically rustic: clumpy boots, loose trousers of a coarse, thick material, and waist-length smocks.

Laedo met their stares with one of his own.

"Is Klystar here?" he demanded loudly.

The labourers scratched their heads and looked questioningly at one another. Then one answered in a polite voice.

"No one of that name in our village. Could you have come to the wrong place?"

Laedo let it pass. "Do you have anyone skilled in metalwork?"

"That's Ebrok the smith you'll be wanting. He makes all our tools and suchlike."

Laedo grunted his disappointment, remembering Hoggora's metalworker on Erspia-1. A village smithy on Erspia-5 would work to about the same standard, he imagined.

He descended the steps. Histrina, with a winsome smile, descended behind him. As her foot touched the turf the local men deferentially fell back, ducking their heads.

"Pleased to meet you, ma'am," they muttered together.

Then they glanced nervously overhead. The man who had answered for them pointed up at the moon.

"You aren't from *there*, are you?" he asked in hushed tones.

"No, we're not from there," Laedo assured him.

He congratulated himself. These people did fear the satellite, as he had guessed. But the local's next words contradicted him.

"I thought not. No one ever comes from there. So where do you come from, in that big . . . contraption you have?"

Laedo steeled himself to deliver incomprehensible information.

"We come from another world, much, much further off than your moon. You know the lights in the sky you see at night? The stars? Those are other worlds."

More scratching of heads. "Well, now, it's hard to see how there could be another *world*. As for the stars, we always thought them the souls of children waiting to be born."

The speaker shook his head and sighed, wearing the amiably confounded expression of one told something remarkable but of little account. "You've come a long way then, by Voluptus, and you'll be needing refreshment, so we'd be failing if we showed you no hospitality. Come along and meet the folks."

All three turned and strolled towards the village without a backward glance to see if their invitation was accepted.

Laedo wondered if it was worthwhile spending any time here, but once again curiosity got the better of him. He beckoned to Histrina, and followed on.

He was struck by a lack of reaction on the part of the farm workers. They accepted his fantastic story with no apparent wish to know more, and with no thought for possible dangers. Was it stupidity, or the habitual placidity of an animal without natural enemies? The inhabitants of Erspia-2 had been like that, and their passivity had hidden a sinister menace. But then they had been genuinely stupid, making no artifacts and with no social organisation. These people had to be smarter—they had an ordered society, built houses, farmed and made tools.

So had Klystar included a rural idyll among his worlds? A peaceful culture without perils or problems? Perhaps as a control culture with which to compare the others . . .

But then there was the business of the moon . . .

In a few minutes they had entered the village, which was arranged around a lush central green shaded by fruit trees. Laedo noted rough dirt roads, scratched out of the landscape by use alone, vanishing into the countryside, presumably leading to other villages.

The atmosphere was tranquil. The timber-framed houses, with their glassless shutter windows, were interspersed with workshops. They passed a cobbler tapping at a nearly-finished boot, his wares laid out under an awning. Nearby was the promised smith, hammering red-hot metal on an anvil. Laedo guessed that the local economy used some form of barter, or even a system of mutual obligations. A number of women were about, accompanied by their children, the girls dressed the same as their mothers in long drab skirts and shapeless blouses, with no attempt at beautification. This was a society where appearances did not matter very much.

Histrina, in a comparatively skimpy shift borrowed from the projector station's supplies, fetched startled glances, even more so than Laedo in his form-fitting duty suit. Her gaze roved over the bodies of the men present, but half-heartedly. They were an unexciting bunch at that, Laedo thought, both men and women.

Still, they were friendly and welcoming. The field labourers' spokesman turned his affable, ingenuous face to Laedo. "My name is Brio Fong. My wife Nellie will have food for us shortly."

Then he made a loud announcement to all within hearing.

"We have visitors from far away! Meet our guests!"

Knowing how suspicious of strangers rural communities could be, Laedo was reassured to see men, women and children wave and smile, the children following their progress with open curiosity. At the end of the village's single street yet more children spilled from the open door of a cottage, running to and fro between the interior and the dusty thoroughfare. "Behave now, children!" Brio Fong cried jovially. "Remember your manners in front of guests!"

And indeed the children did fall quiet, lining up and watching in fascination as Laedo and Histrina were ushered into the cottage. In a cosy but disordered room, a thin woman with a drawn face was stirring a large pot hung over an open fire. From it came an appetising smell of stew.

"Put food on the table, Nellie!" Brio ordered with gusto. "Our friends have come a long way! They are hungry!"

Nellie Fong regarded the newcomers with interest. "Then you are not from Crosshatch, or Bubblespring, or any village nearby? Indeed I don't think I've seen you before."

Brio laughed chidingly. "Why no, woman! They are not from a village at all! They come from the sky and floated down on Butterfly Meadow! In a sort of, er, flying house, I suppose you could call it."

Awe and fright came to Nellie's bony face. The wooden spoon almost dropped from her fingers. "From the sky! You're not from the Heavenly Mansion?"

Again Brio chortled. "No, no, no, woman! Nobody ever comes from there! Our guests hail from even further off! From the other worlds! The worlds in the sky! You know about those, surely?"

"Worlds in the sky?" echoed Nellie.

"Of course! What a patch of befuddlement you are, girl!"

Nellie stared blankly, then appeared to dismiss the matter. Her face cleared. "Well, as long as you love and serve our Lord Voluptus, I suppose that's all right."

With that, she returned to the stewpot.

"Who is this 'Voluptus'?" Laedo enquired politely. "That's the second time I have heard the name today."

Brio, Nellie and their several children gasped and seemed astounded by his words. Nellie was the first to recover herself. "You mean you don't worship the Lord Voluptus?"

"I'm afraid not," said Laedo, slightly taken aback. "We have never heard of him."

Nellie laid down her spoon, straightened herself and faced them with hands on hips. "Then what a mercy it is that you have come to us, poor heathen savages that you are—shoo, children, shoo! Out and play!"

Arms windmilling, she drove the young ones from the house and slammed the door behind them. "Not heard of Voluptus? How could one imagine such a thing! Though there is the tale of the village of Molem in olden times, all of whose people turned their backs on Voluptus. Well! It is up to us to put you right!"

Nellie was clearly in the grip of religious zeal. "The Lord Voluptus is the source of all our blessings. He makes the crops to grow, and the beasts of the field to bear their young. Yes, and the people, too! There would be no one left in the world if he did not bestow children on us. Now anyone may easily see for themselves that Voluptus is real, for you can see his Heavenly Mansion floating up in the sky." With a frown she added, "I suppose you can see it from your world, too?"

Laedo answered with a vague wave of his hand. "What happened to the people of Molem?"

Brio spoke up. "Why, the Lord Voluptus gathered them to his bosom, to show his forgiveness."

That sounded to Laedo like a distorted memory of forcible mass transportation to Erspia-5's tiny moon, some time in the past.

But for what purpose? Was Voluptus an alternative name for Klystar? He recalled how the projector station had seemed to hesitate on passing the moon, as if about to land on it. The place might be worth investigating.

"There's no question about it, you must stay until the Festival of Light," Nellie Fong was saying. "It's only two days away. Then you can go home and explain to everyone there how wonderful it is to adore our benefactor."

Her face became suddenly stern. She cast a disapproving glance at Histrina before stepping to a chest against a wall and lifting the lid. "You'll give our menfolk indecent thoughts dressed like that, my dear. Here, put this on."

She drew out a gown of a drab brown colour, long-skirted and long-sleeved, holding it up for a rough fitting before handing it over. Histrina fingered the thick cloth, shrugged, then drew it over her head, fumbling to fasten the buttons in the front.

Inspecting herself, she tittered.

"This is almost like Courhart!"

"Is that the name of your village?" Nellie responded fussily. "How pleasant it is to be reminded of home."

Laedo noticed a sudden sadness in Histrina's face, an expression he had not seen there before. Brio Fong urged them to the long plank table, shuffling his shoulders in ebullient fashion. "We are all in Voluptus's hands. Is the meal ready, Nellie my dear?"

"Ready it is, husband. Let us adults eat first. The children can come in later."

"Please, I hope you are not giving us your children's supper," Laedo protested anxiously.

"Oh, there's no need for that!" she assured him. "Lord Voluptus gives us full crops and abundant cattle! Our children never go hungry, and what a blessing it is to have them. But don't love the third one."

She said the last absent-mindedly, as if repeating a piece of popular wisdom. They ate from wooden dishes, washing the food down with mugs of an unfamiliar hot beverage which tasted sweet and peppery at the same time. Then the children were allowed back in. There were five of them, three girls and two boys ranging in age from about three to about ten or eleven. Laedo's eye fell on the third eldest. She was a silent, pale-faced girl of six or seven, dressed in a grubby smock. Something about her was different from the others. She was more subdued, more isolated. She came and stood silently by Laedo's knee, as if seeking to draw comfort from a stranger.

Don't love the third one. It was an odd saying. But then, rural cultures had many strange sayings drawn from ancient legends, with no particular contemporary meaning.

He put the matter from his mind and watched the young members of the family eat. The scene was refreshingly normal, after everything he had seen on other Erspian worlds.

Once they had eaten the children were allowed to play indoors for a while, and then were packed off upstairs to bed. Laedo thanked his hosts and announced that he and Histrina would return to their spacecraft.

Brio Fong would hear none of it. He explained that the villagers liked to congregate in the evenings, in what sounded like a cross between a community hall and a tavern. Nellie insisted she would stay indoors in case the children needed her. Laedo and Histrina followed Brio through the front door.

Sunset was not a drawn-out process on any of the Erspia worlds. As they left the cottage the little sun slipped rapidly below the nearby horizon and darkness fell like a curtain.

The half-moon was high in the sky and cast a pale silvery light. Laedo had visited Earth, and had seen the moon gazing down from the night sky there. The scene here was uncannily similar; for the moon appeared about the same size in the sky as on Earth, though its surface was without markings.

Brio told them that the moon passed overhead six times a day. Laedo assumed its orbital speed was controlled artificially, rather than dictated by the equally artificial gravity of its primary. The relatively high rate of orbital revolution would make sense if the moon was being used for surveillance of Erspia-5's surface.

But you wouldn't need a seven-mile-diameter moon in order to do that.

The community hall was crowded. Everyone was curious about the new arrivals. The hall itself was large and comfortable, provided with alcoves, benches and tables. Illumination was the same as in the Fongs's cottage: oil lamps which gave out a warm glow and somewhat smelly fumes. At one end stood a counter, from which a mildly alcoholic beverage was dispensed. No currency was exchanged, but the bartender chalked tallies on wooden boards. Laedo congratulated himself on having guessed correctly. This was a no-money economy.

He and Histrina received mugs of the beverage—called 'beer'—gratis, either on the house or on the tally of some villager or other. Soon they settled into a pleasantly relaxed mood. Laedo let Histrina do most of the talking. This was easy, since the villagers found her the more fascinating of the two. He had to admit that a pretty girl who had dropped out of the sky was more of a draw than a disgruntled middle-aged man, even when he also had dropped out of the sky.

The Erspians were eager to know about the world Histrina came from. A world from beyond their moon was a novel concept. She described it as pretty much like their own, then went on to speak of the worship of the Good Lord.

It was as though she had temporarily forgotten about the evil Ahriman, her master of late. The Good Lord was, she said, the source of everything that was wholesome and pleasant. One only had to follow him to live a happy life.

She might as well have been preaching a sermon by an Ormazdian priest. "Tush, and Brio told us you knew nothing of Voluptus!" exclaimed a plump woman who was the wife of a man called Gollopy. "That's Voluptus you are speaking of, surely."

"No, his name isn't Voluptus," Histrina replied doubtfully. "He has a name, a secret name, though it isn't really secret, which we are told to call upon in times of temptation. I don't know if I ought to tell it to you, but it's Ormazd."

The name mystified them. "I'm sure it must be Voluptus by another name," Gollopy's wife said fussily. "Can you see the Heavenly Mansion from where you live?"

"That big round light in the sky? No, we don't have one of those, just a sun." Histrina frowned. "Of course, there's the other god, Ahriman. He makes you want to do wicked things and tries to turn you against the Good Lord."

There was a pause. "Then it must have been he who corrupted the people of Molem in olden times," someone else said. "But don't worry, your god of wickedness has no disciples here. Perhaps he wouldn't be known on your world, either, if you lived closer to the Heavenly Mansion."

A troubled look came over Histrina. She changed the subject. "Do you know what happens when you die? If you have listened to the Good Lord during your life then your soul goes to paradise and you are given everlasting happiness. But if you gave yourself over to Ahriman then you have everlasting torment." She shuddered and seemed to shrivel. Laedo found the spectacle remarkable.

"Oh but you're wrong there, my dear," Gollopy's talkative wife assured her. "Anyone lucky enough to be one of Voluptus's favourites goes to the Heavenly Mansion, and for them it *is* the Mansion of Pleasure where they do live forever, that's true. But as for the rest of us, well, one lifetime of blessings is enough. It would be ungrateful to expect more."

Histrina only looked confused on hearing this. Laedo thought it unusual for a primitive culture not to have some conception of life after death. Perhaps it went along with the villagers' contentment, their lack of excitement and absence of anything more than superficial curiosity. Many of them spoke of having walked out to Butterly Meadow to view the projector station. Apart from its awesome size they simply saw it as a dull-coloured lump, its metal surface scored and pitted as it was by micrometeorites. Its stated role as a vehicle for travelling between worlds fell flat in their imaginations.

Laedo sighed to himself. Perhaps a life without change or stress was best after all.

Despite offers of shelter for the night, he persuaded Histrina to return to the station. Saying goodnight to their new friends, they staggered in tipsy fashion across the meadow. The moon was once again lifting itself above the horizon. To Laedo's surprise Histrina took his hand in hers as they walked along. In the main lounge, she threw off the drab all-covering gown and threw herself on a couch.

"It's funny," she said, "I don't feel the way I have been feeling lately."

Her voice was subdued, almost plaintive.

"What do you mean?" Laedo asked.

"Well, all that . . . dreadfulness. The bad things I've done. The people I've killed. I don't feel like doing such things any more."

He looked at her quizzically, recalling his earlier idea that the murder and suicide rays might have burned the badness out of her.

Or maybe she was just exhausted. He couldn't take anything for granted.

"What about fornication?" he asked her. "Do you still want to do that?"

She blinked. "I don't see why not."

"You seemed to think it's almost as bad as murder before."

"Did I? I don't know why. What harm does it do? I wouldn't like to do the other things any more, though."

Invitingly she smiled at him.

But he was tired.

And still not sure of Histrina.

He yawned. They slept separately.

He awoke late next day. If Erspia-5 followed the pattern of the other Erspias it had a day of twenty-eight hours. For some still unexplained reason this more accurately represented the natural sleeping and waking cycle of human beings than did the home planet Earth's day of twenty-four hours. Which meant that Laedo had slept long indeed. He recognised that he was getting tired: a tiredness born of frustration.

Still, that frustration might be coming to an end. It could be that Erspia-5's moon would be the end of the projector station's manic search.

He had eaten breakfast before he discovered that Histrina was not in any of the sleeping chambers. The gown given her by Nellie Fong was missing, too. She had left the station.

Outside, men worked in the fields, as before. They waved to him. Brio Fong was not among them, however. Laedo walked into the village and took himself to the Fongs's house.

The two youngest Fong children were playing on the doorstep. The door was ajar. Laedo knocked politely and peered within.

Histrina was already there, assisting Nellie, who was dressing the quiet young girl Laedo had noticed the day before. She was clearly being prepared for a special occasion, not in everyday wear, but in a shiny dress of bright colours, flounces and frills. The two older children were sitting beside their father, watching in silence.

The girl in the dress appeared to be almost in a state of shock.

"We're getting Helsey ready for the Festival of Light!" Histrina announced gaily as Laedo entered.

"Oh, indeed, this is her special day," Nellie Fong added with pride, fussing with pins and tucks.

So that was it. The girl had been chosen to play a role in a religious ceremony. Evidently she was nervous of the attention she was to receive, which to a shy young girl could be intimidating.

Don't love the third one. Laedo thought he had an explanation now. There must be a myth or legend which made every third child especially favoured by Voluptus, so much so that it rendered the parents' love almost superfluous.

The fitting finished, Nellie combed out Helsey's long, fair hair and tied it with ribbons. Brio and the older children clapped and complimented her. She did indeed look pretty, but Laedo wished she would smile occasionally.

Helsey was put back in her drab brown smock while Nellie settled down to stitch the tucks in the ceremonial dress. Brio had taken the day off from his work and cuddled and hugged his daughter often, in a touching display of affection.

"You *are* attending the Festival yourselves, aren't you?" Nellie insisted to Laedo and Histrina. "After all, it only comes once a year."

Laedo assumed the years were measured by the harvests, unless Klystar had arranged a climatic cycle for Erspia-5, which was unlikely.

"Of course!" Histrina promised eagerly.

Fatalistically Laedo agreed. Some time soon he wanted to visit the planetoid's moon, but he was in no hurry.

Despite Histrina's apparent good behaviour, he kept an eye on her for the rest of the day. Once or twice he attempted to engage Helsey in conversation, but the child seemed to have developed a need to be no more than a foot or two away from at least one of her parents: a clinging desire more typical of a worried two year old.

As ever the Fongs were all hospitality, gladly including their guests in the midday meal, which was a lamb roast lovingly prepared by Nellie, accompanied by mixed vegetables and followed by a sweet pudding. The afternoon became an idyllic family scene. Laedo more than once observed Brio wipe a tear from his eye as he watched his daughter being fussed over by her mother. Whenever Helsey looked particularly strained, Nellie would stroke her hair and whisper in her ear, at which the child would utter a relieved giggle, only to relapse into silent sadness shortly afterwards.

The regular work of the community finished early that day. Instead an activity was undertaken on a grassy field, on the opposite side of the village from Butterfly Meadow. A platform was erected, overlain with a deep blue cloth. Meantime straw was carried from a barn and spread all over the field.

Consequently there was no congregating in the drinking hall that evening. Laedo and Histrina retired to the projector station, talked for a while, then slept.

The next day dawned warm and bright. There had been no rain to wet the straw or spoil the proceedings—a fact of which the villagers seemed to have been aware in advance. Brio had advised them that the main ceremony would take place at midmorning. After that, he added, with a brief twinkle in his eye, the festival would begin.

Following a leisurely breakfast, Laedo and Histrina set off. The village was deserted, every door closed. From the distance they could hear music, and on coming to the meadow, saw musicians on the blue-clad platform. There were two violins, a large wooden flute, and a type of harmonium. Though not played very expertly, the instruments achieved an organ-like effect, reminding Histrina of the sort of music that was played in the chapel in her own village of Courhart. The entire adult population of the village was by now trampling the hay that was strewn on the meadow, but surprisingly Laedo could see no children in the crowd. The musicians finished their session and were replaced on the platform by a plump, round-faced man in an untypical garb of scarlet knee breeches and purple waistcoat. Raising his face to the sky, he began to harangue in a nearly shouting voice.

"Lord Voluptus! We thank you for your many gifts! Forgive us our sins, and guide us so that we may know your love in our hearts! Receive now the service of our little ones and bestow upon us the pleasure of your beneficence!"

There was more in the same vein, and Laedo soon stopped listening to it. He noted that the moon, putative dwelling place of Voluptus, had moved directly overhead. At length the speaker concluded his prayer, lowered his head, and gestured into the crowd.

The only children to be present, Helsey and three others around the same age, were brought forward and lifted on to the platform, where they stood together in a line: two little girls and two little boys, all finely turned out in their special clothes. The gathering fell back, creating a space in front of the platform. Laedo could see the Fongs near the front. Their faces were pinched and strained.

Dead silence prevailed, until suddenly one of the boys began to blubber. The composure of the others broke at this. Helsey Fong imploringly held out her arms.

"Mommy! Daddy! I don't want to go! I want to stay with you!"

No reply came. The air around the children was misting, forming a bubble about each of them. Amazingly, their feet lifted off the platform. They were levitating, like puppets being raised up on strings.

The movement was slow at first, but very soon it accelerated. The children were whipped up into the sky.

Towards the moon.

In seconds they had dwindled and disappeared.

Don't love the third one. Laedo now realized how wrong his explanation had been. The saying was not a meaningless relic of some half-remembered legend. It was a response to a real situation. Disease-ridden societies of the past, with high infant mortality, had preached a similar wisdom: don't love your children until they reach the age of ten. Because at least half of them will be dead before then.

The Fongs were relaxed now that the ordeal was over. The tension was gone from their faces. Brio was uncommunicative, but confirmation came easily from the talkative Nellie. Every family's third child was elevated to the Heavenly Mansion of Pleasure on reaching the age of seven, and lived there in perfect happiness, forever and ever. Just what that happiness consisted of was vague. "Oh, every kind of delight and pleasure," was all Nellie would say. "But above all, how wonderful to serve the Lord Voluptus!"

She took pride in asserting that Helsey had always known she was special and a favourite of Voluptus, and that she was destined to leave her family and go to the Heavenly Mansion. Like every other third child, it had been impressed on her how fortunate she was.

If Laedo was any judge, Helsey did not want to be special, or fortunate.

He drew away from the others and rejoined Histrina, who was gazing up at the palely shining satellite.

"What goes on up there, do you think?"

"Maybe we could go and take a look."

"It was incredible the way they shot up into the sky!"

Laedo smiled wryly. The children's spectacular ascent was simply one more application of the exquisite control of inertial fields exhibited on all the Erspia worlds. After everything he had seen, transferring someone to the orbiting moon in a self-enclosed bubble of air was no great trick.

Others were looking upwards too. The crowd, which had given rise to a subdued hubbub, fell silent again.

The phenomenon known as the Festival of Light began.

It was as though the sky was a canvas to which an artist was applying washes of colour one after another. First came a translucent mauve which streamed down as though spreading through blotting paper. Then came a similar wash of a clear, glasslike cerise, followed by saffron, a shining lemon yellow, a delightful light green, and a pale purple. Without pause the waves of coloured light sifted down and in seconds were falling on the meadow.

The crowd mooed with anticipation, and as the changing colours phased, the scene was transformed. Laedo found his perceptions altering, subtly at first, then to a startling degree. Outlines became sharper, colours brighter but at the same time softer. The people around him were as if seen under the influence of a psychedelic drug, or as if they were in a surrealist painting. Reality had altered. Time had slowed. His skin tingled.

The tingling was only a premonition. After about a minute his body exploded with pleasure. Erotic desire seized hold of him and shook him like a tree in the wind.

This was not an influence imposed from without, as with Klystar's thought beams. It welled up from within, as though every sexual desire he had ever experienced thus far was no more than a seeping or leaking from a dam which now had burst.

Pleasure . . . pleasure . . . the coloured light *was* pleasure. The pleasure was the light. He moved in pleasure as a fish swims in water. There was music, too, music which loosened the heart and melted all restrictions—but when he listened closely, there was no music, his brain was inventing it in his delirium. Not far away he saw Nellie Fong. Her eyes were glazed, her face in a sulk of prurience. She was fumbling with the buttons and hooks of her long drab gown. Soon it was sliding from her to fall in a heap on the ground. Beneath it she wore an equally long and rather grubby shift. That, too, slid off, and Nellie Fong, prim and proper middle-aged wife and mother, stood naked on the spread straw.

Previously her scrawny body and wasted breasts could only have repelled Laedo. Now he was filled with an irresistible need to use her. Without even realizing it he had cast off his utility garment and was also naked. He and Nellie eyed one another, then came together. A sour reek came from her, but that only excited him all the more. She ground her pudendum against him, her breath coming in gasps, but that was not what he wanted. He grabbed her by the haunches, turned her back to him, seized her thin wrists in one hand and pushed her arms up, forcing her to bend over. Her narrow, almost fleshless buttocks angled up at him. Roughly he plunged his stiffened phallus into her revealed anus. He seemed to feel her glorious pain as he delivered vigorous thrusts. The orgasm, when it came, sent spears of sapphire brilliance flashing like jagged lightning behind his eyeballs.

He pushed her off his phallus and sent her sprawling face-first on the straw. Everyone around him either had or was disrobing. Scenes of maddened carnality were unfolding. The meadow was caught within a rainbow, colour succeeding colour, melding and mixing, each colour bringing even more intense pleasure. The air was filled with what his mind interpreted as strident orchestral music, but which in actuality was a cacophony of shouts, mewlings, grunts and screams. He saw Brio Fong in boisterous coitus with Histrina. Then, before he knew it, he had become part of a squirming mass of bodies pressing and sliding against one another, male and female. He had taken pleasure-enhancing drugs before, but this was ecstasy such as he had never imagined, another universe in which hands, feet, legs, arms, bellies, buttocks, chests, backs, lips, genitals, were only there for the sake of excitement and voluptuousness.

At some point he again saw Nellie Fong. She was in the midst of a heap or knot composed of herself and ten men. Her stick-like legs were splayed at an extraordinarily lewd angle.

Two distended penises were stuffed into her vagina, two up her anus. She was boggle-eyed at the two more being crammed into her grossly distended mouth, while she also gripped two in each fist, pumping them in alternating pistoning motions.

Then she was lost to view amid roiling flesh. After what seemed like years spent in eternity, but which in clock time was about two hours, the mellifluous curtains of colour faded. Mundane reality returned. The moon was low on the horizon. Golden, glorious bodies became, for the most part, the lumpen forms of village dwellers who picked themselves up dazed and exhausted, and began looking for their clothing.

Where were the village children while the orgy was in progress? Presumably locked away in their houses safe from adult goings-on. The waves of light would be restricted to the designated meadow and similar meadows across Erspia-5.

And the 'third ones'? Laedo now was wondering just what kind of 'services' they were required to perform in the Heavenly Mansion.

SEVEN

Moon of Doom

"That was fantastic!" Histrina exclaimed. "Even better than the orchids!"

"I must admit I enjoyed it too," Laedo agreed. "But it's still manipulation."

They were in the projector station's living quarters. Their return from the 'Festival of Light' had left them still somewhat aroused, and they had continued erotic practices with one another for a while. Then they had fallen asleep.

It was now the following day. Laedo was considering what to do next. He was half convinced that 'Voluptus' was in fact Klystar, and that Erspia-5's moon was his dwelling place.

Of course, he only had the word of the Guardians of Ormazd that there *was* a being called Klystar at all. But someone had fashioned the Erspia worlds. Whoever it was possessed a technology in advance of mankind's.

What kept the Erspia worlds together as a group, for instance? They were in interstellar space and should have drifted apart. Artificial inertial fields—those known to human technology, at any rate—acted over short distances only. Yet the planetoids were thousands of miles apart, and had remained grouped together for a century at least.

Would the projector station head for the moon if he again asked it to take him to Klystar? Perhaps, but perhaps not. If he wanted to see the moon, a better bet would be to use his own cargo ship.

Should he be thinking of visiting the moon at all? Should he not get down to gaining control of the projector station's drive? There was no guarantee of success there either. While the station seemed fairly simple technically, 'Klystar' had very likely made sure the human Guardians of Ormazd could not seize control of it prematurely. For that matter, he didn't know if the station really could reach a human-inhabited world as 'Klystar' had promised.

If only he had a forming machine and the right grade of

steel, he could probably make a transductor for his cargo ship himself . . .

But in the end he had to admit that getting home was no longer his sole motive. He had seen five experiments in social engineering where human beings were treated as though they were ants in a formicarium.

He wanted to know what it was all about.

"All right, Histrina," he said, "do you want to visit the Heavenly Mansion?"

Eagerly she agreed. "If the Festival of Light was so good, think what the Mansion of Pleasure must be like!"

"Don't count on it," he told her. "That was a bribe, one good enough to persuade people to give up their children—with some religious propaganda thrown in."

The first problem was to secure the projector station during their absence, though he imagined the villagers would be too polite to enter it uninvited. The portal had no manual locking mechanism on the outside. Instead, as he had ascertained during his first encounter, it responded to a radio code. He and Histrina transferred to the cargo ship. He lifted from the surface of the station, descended until the hatch came in view, and transmitted a brief burst. The hatch obediently closed.

Laedo again touched the controls. The cargo ship ascended into the sky on its manoeuvring engine, quickly traversing the atmosphere. The stars appeared and the tiny sun blazed hard without the softening effect of the air blanket. The moon, which on take-off had been heading for the horizon, lay ahead, glowing in the light of the sun and three quarters gibbous, a mellow, yellow-white globe.

Still using the manoeuvring engine, Laedo flew close to the tiny world. Its atmosphere, visible as a radiant nimbus, appeared to be deeper than the atmospheres of the Erspia worlds themselves, but then he realized that this was an illusion produced by the moon's smaller diameter. The air had to be deep enough to have a breathable density at ground level.

"The Mansion of Heavenly Pleasure," Histrina breathed, her eyes shining. "I can't wait!"

"I told you not to anticipate things, Histrina," Laedo rebuked. "Whatever's down there *won't* be what you expect. Haven't you learned that by now?"

"Oh, you always want to spoil things."

They entered the atmosphere and descended in a shallow dive. A curved landscape showed itself. Features appeared: low rolling hills, isolated valleys and canyons. Mostly, though, the moon consisted of a level plain, dull yellow in colour. Laedo got the impression it was coated with yellow moss.

Oddly, he saw no open water. No rivers, lakes or seas. Cloud was rare, a few wispy streaks. Neither did he see any growing crops or herds of animals. If there was any sizeable population it did not appear to support itself by farming or hunting.

There *was* a population, however. The cargo ship came in sight of what could only be described as a set of fabulous palaces. Histrina *oohed* and *aahed* as they circled the complex from the air. Pavilions, domes, classical frontages, all sparkled in the air.

Then Laedo spotted something which had been hidden from him at first, partly by the curvature of the landscape and also because it was concealed in a declivity. It was an enormous long shape lying on its side. Steering so as to hover over the object, Laedo was startled. Though old, battered and dented, its metal skin scored, stained and pitted, the structure was still recognisable.

It was an interstellar passenger liner. But how old? One century? Two? Dropping lower, Laedo managed to read the worn, patchy name on the liner's flank.

IFS Excelsior.

It took him a few moments to remember where he had heard the name. "The *Excelsior,*" he murmured. "Didn't a ship of that name disappear *en route*, early last century? They never did find her, did they?"

He shook his head in irritation with himself. He was absent-mindedly asking Histrina questions she knew nothing about. She was gazing blankly at the image of the liner. After the wonders she had seen lately it made little impression on her.

Even though, if Laedo was guessing correctly, her ancestors were among the *Excelsior*'s passengers and crew. A vital question had been answered.

The missing starliner must be the source of Klystar's original human stock.

He was about to move off when a slight movement caught his attention. A figure had emerged from the hulk and was waving frantically up at the cargo ship.

Laedo immediately took his vessel down and landed a short distance away. "Wait here," he said. "I'm going outside."

In seconds he was standing on the surface of Erspia-5's moon. The air smelled fresh, with a faint tang of lemon. As he had thought, a springy yellow moss was underfoot, but there was no time to examine it more closely. The man from the starliner ran up to him.

"Thank God you've come at last!"

Laedo stared at the stranger, who like himself wore a dark-coloured utility suit. He was stocky, with intense brown eyes, his broad face fringed with black hair and a black spade beard. His demeanour was agitated. It struck Laedo that his cast of face was not at all like that of Erspians generally.

Narrow yellow stripes adorned the shoulders of his suit. A badge of rank, most likely.

"My name's Garo," he gasped. "I'm the Excelsior's purser. How many others are coming? Is there a warship on the way? Tell me, for God's sake!"

Laedo swallowed. "Calm yourself," he mumbled. Then he cleared his throat and spoke up.

"I'm sorry, but no one else is coming. I am a Class CCC cargo carrier, but I am stranded, like you. My main drive has a cracked transductor."

The other's shoulders sagged. He groaned and turned aside. "Will rescue never come?"

Laedo had a question. "Did you say you are the ship's purser? Excuse me, but the *Excelsior* vanished long ago. How are you still alive?"

"That's simple enough. I've spent the time in a stasis cabinet. I'm the only one to have escaped Klystar's clutches."

"Then there *is* a Klystar?" Laedo's eyes widened.

"Oh, there's a Klystar all right," Garo confirmed bitterly. "You'll find that out. He took all the others and used them for breeding stock. I spent five days hiding in a sewer conduit. When the ship was empty I came out and took to the cabinet. He knows I'm here but he leaves me alone—after all, I'm almost never around. I come out and take a look every few years, and I've an alarm rigged to detect any ship that arrives. Rescue *must* come some day."

Laedo considered this. A stasis cabinet was a by-product of the star drive. It could slow down time within it. The past century and a half could have been only weeks or days to Garo. Events of long ago would seem of recent occurrence to him.

"Is Klystar here?" he asked. "On this moon?"

Garo reacted nervously to the question. "Yes, he's here."

"Can't you use the *Excelsior* to get home?"

"No, Klystar saw to that. He junked the star drive and pretty well everything else. I've enough power to run some lighting and the stasis cabinet. And I've food to last. But that's all."

"Tell me about Klystar."

"What is there to tell? He's a monster! But you'll see for yourself. There's nowhere for you to go."

Garo shot a sudden glance over Laedo's shoulder. He went pale. "Here he comes now. I'd better make myself scarce."

Laedo turned to look. A tall 'something' had appeared over the nearby horizon. It walked on two long, thin legs, themselves as tall as a man. The body was stubby, the head cylindrical.

Garo was running for the *Excelsior*. Laedo hesitated. Should he return to his ship and stick with Histrina?

But that would avail little against the almost omnipotent Klystar. Laedo wanted more information. He decided to follow Garo. Scrambling through a service hatch in pursuit of the ex-purser, he found himself in a dimly lit corridor. Looking back, Garo saw him, but shrugged and went on.

The *Excelsior* was a ghost ship. Corridors and salons boomed to the sound of their footsteps. The air smelled stale. Eventually Garo descended a companionway to a store room in which lay rows of cargo containers. One of them had been opened. What it had contained stood alongside: a cabinet or chamber with a transparent front. And visible within it, a straight-backed chair.

This was the stasis cabinet. The chief use of such a device was to preserve a mortally injured person until medical help could arrive. Occasionally someone would use it to transfer himself to a future century, a less risky procedure than cryogenic freezing. Garo had been lucky to find one among the ship's cargo.

"Look," said Garo, turning to Laedo, "this is the only stasis cabinet on the ship, and you can see there's only room for one in it. If you get your ship working, please come and get me. I assume you'll do that, with your ethical rating. Otherwise I suggest you make your way to one of the pleasure palaces. They'll look after you there."

"What happens in these palaces?" Laedo asked.

Garo looked at him for a moment. "The people there are servants of Klystar. They just sort of keep things running. The young children who arrive are mostly assigned to sexual duties with the older servants. Paedophilia is a way of life here, I don't know why. Later they learn general duties."

He paused before continuing in a sombre tone. "Those are the lucky ones. Others are assigned to Klystar's special project." He shuddered slightly as he turned to enter the cabinet. "I don't want to talk about that. I told you he's a monster."

Laedo put a hand on his arm to detain him. "Wait. Tell me more. What exactly happened to the *Excelsior?*"

"Klystar seized her, of course, what do you think? Don't ask me how he did it. He gained remote control and brought her here, then took everybody off and put them on the worlds he made. It's some kind of experiment of his. Then he wrecked the engines and nearly everything else."

"How many Erspia worlds are there?"

"I'm not sure. About ten, I think, not counting this moon."

"What keeps them so close together?"

"Are you stupid? They're in a Trojan orbit. There are two brown dwarfs, orbiting half a light year apart, one bigger than the other. The Erspia group forms an equilateral triangle with them."

Laedo nodded. It was a much simpler explanation than he had imagined. Like the Trojan asteroids sharing the orbit of Jupiter, the Erspia worlds would be prevented from drifting away by the combined attractions of the two brown dwarfs, drawn back whenever they began to deviate. It was the only stable fixed configuration of three bodies permissible under gravitational influence.

He had not been aware of the presence of the brown dwarfs, which would be invisible to the eye. But his ship's navigator had probably spotted them and made a course correction.

"The Erspians don't seem to know anything about their origins," he commented.

"Of course not!" The remark exasperated Garo. "It would spoil the experiment if they did, wouldn't it? Do you suppose Klystar isn't able to fix that?"

Garo was becoming increasingly nervous, glancing frequently at the stasis cabinet. He seemed to feel he was only safe when inside it.

Which was silly. Klystar would be able to turn it off at any time. Even Laedo would be able to, if it came to that.

"Anything else you want to know!" Garo shouted.

When Laedo didn't answer, he opened the door of the cabinet and stepped inside.

It was fascinating to watch the relativistic time dilation effect take hold. The instant Garo closed the door behind him his movements began to slow. They continued to slow progressively, until by the time he had seated himself on the straight-backed chair he was virtually immobile.

Laedo turned away. It was time to face Klystar.

Cautiously he emerged from the *Excelsior* and was shocked to find Klystar confronting him only a few yards away.

The alien loomed over the Harkio man. The spindly legs stood as high as Laedo's shoulders. The earlier impression of a squat torso was confirmed. There were four arms, which were also long and spindly. The head was a turret, with a row of five eyes.

Klystar wore no clothing or artificial covering that Laedo could see. His body was yellow and slightly shiny. There was no sign of genitals. Then was Klystar a robot? No, Laedo decided, he was of organic origin. The shiny integument was a chitin-like substance.

After everything he had seen of Klystar's handiwork, Laedo found that he was awed and unable to speak or act.

The turret head rotated with deliberation, in little jerks. Each eye regarded Laedo in turn. Using immaculate Argot Galactica, though in a rather reedy voice, Klystar spoke.

"Were you talking with Garo?"

"Yes."

"He can't help you. He is like a mite living in the wall, who comes out to eat flakes of dead skin."

Klystar's head rotated again. He was examining the cargo ship.

Then he strode away, on the same course he had been following when Garo first sighted him. Soon he had disappeared over the horizon, as though walking down a stairway and out of sight.

Laedo made up his mind. He would call Klystar to account, superhuman though his technology might be. He scurried after the enigmatic alien.

On reaching the point where Klystar had vanished, he found himself looking down into a broad, shallow valley ringed by an almost continuous ridge, like a ring crater. In the ridge was a gap opening on to a sloping path, and down this Klystar was walking.

The valley contained signs of habitation. There were swathes given over to the cultivation of grain crops—a feature absent on the rest of the moon—and rows of barrack-like dwellings.

More prominent, and distinctly puzzling to Laedo's mind, was that scattered about the crater were piled-up heaps of tumbled masonry, apparently the collapsed ruins of grand monuments. At the sound of Laedo's steps, Klystar stopped. His cylindrical head rotated a hundred and eighty degrees, like an owl's. The middle one of his five eyes regarded Laedo, who walked closer and stared up at the unhuman face in challenge.

"Why do you carry out experiments on human beings?" he demanded in as loud a voice as he could manage. "Don't you know it's wrong?"

Klystar's head turned slightly, bringing the second eye from the left into line with Laedo. Another turn, and the second eye from the right regarded him. Then the extreme left eye, followed by the extreme right eye.

Laedo was intrigued. Did Klystar's perceptions alter according to the order in which he used his eyes?

"Wrong?" Klystar echoed, his tone heavy with scepticism. "What is the meaning of 'wrong'?"

"Ethically wrong. Surely you know what ethical means. It is not right to use intelligent beings for your own ends, without their knowledge or consent."

Klystar gave vent to a sigh. Laedo wondered where his voice was coming from. He could see no mouth.

"First of all, your species is not intelligent in the proper meaning of the word," Klystar said. "An intelligent being has control over his consciousness. He forms his own thoughts and does not allow others to form them for him. His mental state is not at the disposal of others. This is not so in your case, is it?"

"We are a social species," Laedo argued. "We don't live in isolation. We interact with one another."

"Yes, I am familiar with your social organisation. It is a feature of the lower orders of life. You are the mammalian parallel of the social insects—ants, bees and termites, to name those that occur on your original Earth. The only difference is that where you are concerned the social phenomenon incorporates a mild degree of intellectual functioning. But no human being would have any intellectual functioning at all were he raised outside human society."

"And you would?" Laedo asked in amazement.

"One of my kind, if born and left to develop without any company or education, would grow up fully conscious and with full reasoning ability. That is the case with all the intelligent species which I-Klystar have encountered, with the sole exception of yours. That is why I-Klystar took the trouble to study you. You are a curiosity. You are a species which can think, to some extent, and yet which lacks inner determination."

Klystar's eyes shifted again. "The condition can be attributed to your species having evolved too quickly. Your native biosphere is less than four billion years old. Ten billion years is the normative time frame in which to evolve an intelligent species. A series of accidents on the Earth home world would appear to be responsible for this premature development. Your scientists must have wondered why your galaxy rarely contains anything higher than animal life."

"Yes, they have," Laedo admitted thoughtfully. Klystar was right. The galaxy abounded with life, but nowhere did it get any further than the equivalent of a mouse or a horse or a lizard, or a fish or even a bacterium. And yet many of the biospheres examined were much older than Earth's.

Astronomers had come up with an explanation which tended to agree with Klystar's assertion. The planets and moons of the solar system were heavily cratered as a result of long-term bombardment by asteroids and meteorites. It came as a surprise to discover that the same had not happened to other planetary systems, which had known more peaceful and orderly histories. Something unusual must have happened to the solar system early on. It was now accepted that there really had once been a planet between Mars and Jupiter, and that it had disintegrated, filling the system with dangerous debris. While evolution elsewhere proceeded at a sedate pace, on Earth it had been forced to cope with recurrent catastrophes—mass extinctions from asteroid strikes which sometimes had nearly extinguished the biosphere altogether. The repeated twists and turns of fate had accelerated evolutionary change.

What could have shattered a planet? Collision between neighbouring worlds, while possible, would not have scattered the fragments far and wide, as had happened. They would have slumped back together by self-gravitation. Something more energetic was needed, and for that one had to look outside the solar system. The current hypothesis was that an interstellar intruder, zipping through the solar system with enormous velocity from high above the ecliptic plane, was the culprit.

Collision was more plausible if a cluster of interstellar transients was involved. Another might have struck Uranus a glancing blow, tilting its axis to its present unusual alignment nearly parallel to its orbital plane.

So far so good. But for the accident to have resulted in a premature and half finished mankind, flawed, inadequate, below the cosmic standard, was a new and unwelcome idea.

"Come with me," Klystar said. "I-Klystar will show you what I mean."

He resumed striding down the rubble-strewn slope. Laedo followed. Once they neared the valley floor, the crater's panorama vanished. The horizon intervened, leaving only the lip of the crater wall visible to the eye.

Klystar's approach had been noticed. A crowd of people poured from the barracks and fields to welcome him. They reminded Laedo of primitives on some island paradise, naked except for a simple piece of white cloth worn around the waist, by both men and women. They fell to their knees before Klystar, placing their hands together in an attitude of prayer.

A hoarse, windy voice arose from one of the older men.

"We have buried our dead, O Klystar! How have we failed?"

In a stentorian voice, completely different from the one he had used when speaking to Laedo, Klystar answered.

"YOU HAVE NOT HAD ENOUGH FAITH! BEGIN AGAIN! HAVE MORE FAITH! YOU MUST BEGIN A NEW TOWER TOMORROW!"

A chant grew from the crowd. *"We will have faith! We will begin again!"*

The crowd melted away as the people returned from whence they had come.

"Look at those idiots," Klystar said quietly. With one of his four thin lank arms he pointed to the nearest pile of ruins on the horizon. It appeared to be the base of a tower, surrounded by tumbled stone. "For generations I-Klystar have been telling them to build a tower twenty miles high so that they can climb up it to heaven. It is manifestly impossible to build a tower that high with the materials available. On reaching a certain height it collapses and kills large numbers of the builders. Yet do they ever lose faith in me? Do they tell themselves that I-Klystar might be lying and perhaps am not even a god, as they think? No, they do not. They begin again. And simply because my personality is stronger than theirs."

Such cynicism appalled Laedo. But he was also puzzled. Why should the mighty Klystar, whose deeds were so awesome, come to resemble a corny Jehova?

At the same time there was something odd in the way the alien being referred to himself as 'I-Klystar'. Or was it 'I/Klystar'?

An inspired thought came to him. He blurted it out immediately.

"You're not Klystar at all, are you? What are you? A robot proxy? Or a biological one, perhaps?"

'Klystar' paused, before he answered, his tone neutral and matter-of-fact. "You have acuity, for a member of an inferior race," he congratulated. "No, I-Klystar am not a proxy. I am a relic. To be exact, I am Klystar's body. Klystar himself, that is to say his mind, or essence, is away journeying. Methods for moving material objects, such as those used by your starships, are not fast enough for his requirements. He uses a technique which abstracts the individual from his corporeal form and expresses him as a pattern of consciousness and thought. This can be instantaneously transferred to an immense distance."

"How?"

"By a means known as Immediacy of Thought. It would be tiresome to explain."

"What happens at the other end?"

"A replacement body is needed as an instrument of action. Klystar forms one from available materials where this is possible. Or he may arrange for one to be constructed beforehand."

"How?"

"Again, it would be tiresome to explain."

"Isn't this a risky process? What if he can't get a body?"

"Then he is unable to return. You are right, there is a degree of uncertainty, but Klystar has no fear of destruction. Better to die than to desist from the search for knowledge. Besides, Klystar has lived for over a million years as you measure time, and he has learned to survive most accidental events."

Laedo thought over everything he had been told. "You say you are just a body, without Klystar's mind. But you talk, walk about, appear to be a rational being."

"That is because Klystar's body has remanent intelligence of its own, just as yours does. Were it otherwise, Klystar and yourself would personally have to supervise bodily functions like digestion."

Laedo laughed. "Then you are no different from me! You are inferior too!"

"If you like, but that is exactly the point. Klystar's discarded integument still has more intelligence than does your entire species. In any case, I have been a part of Klystar. That makes a difference."

"And the religious cult you have in this crater? Is that your work?"

"It is my own little experiment in human gullibility."

"I thought so. To be frank, it lacks the grandeur of Klystar's set-ups. You probably didn't even need to use thought-beams.

Human prophets aplenty have made people discard their reason, using nothing more than persuasion and charisma."

"I-Klystar am sure you are right. But what a pity your species is so amenable to these ploys."

Laedo changed the subject. "What happens when Klystar comes back? Will you be reunited with him?"

"No, this body is worn out. A new body will have to be prepared for Klystar's return."

"So what will happen to you?"

"Either Klystar will destroy me or I will simply be left to age and die."

"And when is he coming back?"

"He has been overdue for some time now. Perhaps he has found something of unusual interest, or perhaps he no longer wishes to review the results of his social experiments. There could be many reasons for his lateness."

"Where has he gone?"

"To another galaxy, I believe. I do not know which one."

Laedo was impressed. "Is he native to this galaxy?"

"His kind evolved on a planet of an intergalactic star. Most intelligent beings have a similar origin. Galaxies are generally too young to have produced intelligent life."

Again Laedo paused for thought. "What if Klystar never comes back?"

"The experiments will continue until the suns run out of power. That will be in about three hundred years time."

"Why don't you act on your own initiative?" Laedo challenged. "You could bring this nonsense to an end now."

"You proposal does not make sense. I-Klystar am an aspect of Klystar. Klystar's wishes are law. Would your hand disobey you?"

'Klystar' started back up the slope. Laedo hurried to keep up with him.

"If Klystar meets members of his own species, does he talk to them?" he asked. "Or to members of other fully intelligent species?"

"The latter is more likely since his own species is scattered after so much time. When intelligent beings meet they usually trade knowledge. They have little social interest in one another apart from that."

Laedo reflected that according to what 'Klystar' had said, intelligence must currently be a rare occurrence in the universe, confined to those stars which happened to be older than the galaxies. Yet the time would come when the galaxies themselves burgeoned with intelligence. The older generation would then be eclipsed.

He was reminded of the overthrow of the ancient Titans by the younger gods in Greek myth.

"I wonder if you would do something for me," he said. My ship needs a repair. The replacement of a part which can be manufactured quite easily. Will you help me? Then I can continue my journey and return home."

"I'm afraid I cannot allow you to leave the Erspia worlds," 'Klystar' told him apologetically. "You would summon help and jeopardise the experiment. You will have to spend your remaining days here. Join the staff of one of the pleasure palaces. The time should pass enjoyably enough."

It was the reply Laedo had expected, but it still annoyed him. "Klystar shouldn't have carried out the experiment in the first place!" he retorted. "You should study the doctrine of *karmayoga*. I'll explain it to you. There is a law of nature which applies to our actions, like the law of action and reaction in physics except that it takes longer to work. Everything you do to another being, good or bad, rebounds on you. If you act towards another in a way which is hurtful or harmful, then at some time in the future the consequences of that action will strike you too. Think of the bad karma Klystar is bringing on himself with these experiments!"

"I am already familiar with the *karmayoga* doctrine," 'Klystar' replied. "It involves two errors. Firstly, if the universe is indeed an ethical construct, then the law of *karma* can apply only to fully self-directed beings such as Klystar. Human beings lack inner unity, have only flickering consciousness, and do not control their actions, and therefore cannot be held responsible for those actions. They are ethical blanks."

"All right, but where does that leave Klystar?" Laedo pressed earnestly. "He *is* self-directed!"

"Secondly, the universe is not an ethical construct, anyway," 'Klystar' continued implacably. "There is no law of *karma*.

There is no cosmic retribution. It is one of countless myths the human race has invented in order to delude itself."

Laedo's annoyance turned to anger. "Well, as you're so clever I suppose you must be right, but it's still the law *I* live by! Perhaps there's something you don't know. Perhaps the universe itself evolves by producing conscious creatures. You say Klystar belongs to the first generation of such creatures, spawned between the galaxies from the earliest stars. Perhaps that generation is deficient, primitive in some way, a first attempt. Perhaps the second generation will be better. Perhaps even we poor human beings have qualities which Klystar's kind don't. The law of karma might make its appearance in future ages."

'Klystar' stopped walking, gazing at Laedo, shifting his head to use yet another sequential combination of his five eyes.

"Are you sure that you live according to the philosophy of *karmayoga*?" he enquired politely. "I-Klystar have been aware of your travels. The projector station which you appropriated has been reporting its movements to me. So I-Klystar know that you disengaged the Ormazdian thought beam, leaving only the Ahrimanic beam to irradiate the world below it. Do you realize what horrors you have inflicted on thousands of helpless people by so doing, simply in order to further your own ends? Where is 'right action' in that?"

'Klystar' strode on, but this time Laedo did not follow him. He just stood where he was.

He was stunned.

EIGHT

The Mansion of Pleasure

Laedo couldn't understand why he hadn't thought about this before. He distinctly remembered the moment when, with a mental shrug, he had pulled the lever which switched off the 'good' Ormazdian beam. Since then he had experienced not one flicker of conscience or remorse.

How could a Class CCC cargo carrier, with a corresponding ethical rating, have done such a thing?

Then, too, he had locked Histrina in the radiation safe while he went exploring on Erspia-4, without adequate provision for her plight should he fail to return.

Only one explanation occurred to him. Despite his precautions, the thought beams had affected him. Without his being aware of it, he had become mentally confused.

It was, he conceded ruefully, yet one more confirmation of the human condition so belittled by 'Klystar'.

Could a thought beam affect Klystar himself? Presumably not. It was a question of individuality. Social insects such as ants, bees and termites had none. They could not distinguish one another as individuals, only as members of a caste: worker, drone or warrior. Klystar stood at the other extreme: he was pure individual, able to achieve unaided what would take an entire society of human beings. He had no need of companionship or co-operation.

Mankind stood midway between the two: a social being with some level of intelligence. For that reason human beings were susceptible to thought-moulding.

Laedo asked himself what he could do to remedy his dreadful act. Return the projector station to Erspia-1 and switch the beam back on? He didn't yet know how to do the first. In fact 'Klystar' had made it sound as though he never would be able to take control of the station.

Return to Erspia-1 and remove the Ahrimanic beam? A similar problem presented itself there. His cargo ship had a protective beam weapon, but the manoeuvring engine would not take it to Erspia-1.

Despondently Laedo trudged the rest of the way to his cargo ship. Histrina was still in the lounge, looking at the viewscreen.

"What was that monstrous thing that came walking by?" she asked breathlessly. "That's not a person, is it?"

"That's Klystar. Sort of."

He sat down and became lost in his thoughts.

"Klystar? Who the station keeps chasing? Now it's found him, can we go to Harkio if we want?"

Laedo didn't answer. He had his head in his hands.

Histrina was oblivious of his mood. Her eyes were gleaming. "Let's not go there straight away. *Pleasure palaces*! Let's try those first!"

She jumped to her feet. "Let's go now!"

Laedo raised his heed and looked at the tops of the domes and pavilions which showed over the horizon. There seemed little danger in visiting the palaces. Both Garo and 'Klystar' apparently assumed Laedo would take up residence there of his own accord sooner or later.

Also, he was curious to see the heart of Klystar's operation. "All right."

They left the station together. The walk to the complex took only a few minutes. It was like approaching a theme park or amusement centre. There was a light, airy elegance to the prospect which opened up and expanded the nearer one came. They made for the largest of the palaces and stopped before a grandiloquent entrance flanked by Doric pillars. They cautiously entered a spacious hall with a gleaming tiled floor. People crossed the hall on enigmatic errands, appearing and disappearing through various doorways. All were dressed in loose flowing robes and bore an air of calm.

A tall, slim young man accosted them. "You are strangers," he said in a friendly voice. "Are you from below?"

"That's right," Laedo answered.

"Ah. It is rare for us receive adults." He paused. "You will wish to find places here."

"That depends," Laedo said. "We were not brought here. We came under our own power. If we don't like it we can go back."

The slim man looked puzzled at this statement. Then his face cleared as he dismissed the conundrum. "Oh, you will certainly like it here! No one could prefer the drab world below. It is nearly time for the evening banquet, which I urge you to attend. Such food!"

"Well, can we have a look round?"

"By all means. Later I will assign you quarters and we can discuss your role here."

Still smiling, their host touched two fingers to his brow in a casual gesture of farewell, and went on his way.

Histrina sighed. The great sunny entrance hall, the palace staff quietly going about its business, all had a reassuring quality. It was easy to imagine that life here could be pleasant indeed.

* Then something happened which reminded Laedo of what Garo had said. A group of children ran into the hall, aged perhaps eight to ten, laughing, playing a game of tag. They were completely naked, which made a bizarre contrast with the fact that their faces were heavily made up with lipstick, rouge and eye shadow, both girls and boys.

The group swirled around the two and then were off, disappearing through one of the doorways. A gleeful leer came over Histrina as she realized the import of the children's unclothed cosmetics. She started off towards the way they had gone, only to be restrained by Laedo.

"Later," he placated, sadly aware that he would not be able to deflect Histrina from her lustful nature if they stayed here any length of time.

By now little Helsey Fong was probably running around naked somewhere not far away, available to the older staff members.

Histrina tailed after him as he began the task of exploring the palace. The banqueting hall, already being laid out for the evening repast, was nearby. There were salons, fountained arcades, a huge kitchen, sumptuous boudoirs obviously not designed simply for sleeping, and contrariwise, sleeping quarters.

The question of where the food came from was answered: all the palace's wastes were recycled in sealed biological chambers which cultivated edible tissues directly, both vegetable and animal. Once again Klystar's technology was excellent. The produce was gourmet class.

Mounting a staircase, they emerged on to a balcony giving a view of the surrounding moonscape. The other palaces lay in the light of the low sun, imparted an odd canted appearance by the small moon's curvature.

Turning to quit the balcony, Laedo noticed a long narrow corridor leading to the right. So far he had only been able to see the ground floor of the palace. Obviously there were more floors above it, but this was time he had found access to any of them.

Histrina in tow, he paced the length of the corridor. At its end he found a narrow stairway spiralling upwards. The stair-well was dim as he climbed, having no lights of its own. He and Histrina reached the top and entered a long, windowless gal-lery. Ceiling strips provided lighting. Arranged along the mid-dle of the room were six low tanks or vats, oval in shape. Laedo stepped to the nearest and looked into it. A thick, yellow fluid filled it to just below the rim, pus- or vomit-like and gleaming slightly.

The odour which came off the stuff seemed to shift as Laedo tried to identify it. Now it smelled like hot plastic, now like blood, now like toffee. He glanced to the other tanks. Something was happening in the adjacent one. The fluid rippled, swirled, smoothed out, then humped up. A form emerged, like a naiad rising from a pond. A little girl, looking wanly about her.

It was Helsey Fong. She was bare of the cosmetics worn by the children running about below, but she was just as naked. The vision persisted only for a few seconds. Her substance melted and flowed back into the vat.

Laedo put together what Garo had said about Klystar's special project, and what 'Klystar' had said about the ancient alien's need for a new body. So this was the special project. This was what happened to those children who were not 'the lucky ones'. They were melted down to provide living substance from which to make a new body for the returning Klystar.

Garo was right. Klystar *was* a monster.

At the far end of the gallery a very tall door slid open with a *click*. 'Klystar' strode through, head rotating rapidly from side to side, bringing each of his eyes to the fore in turn.

Histrina scurried for the stairway. Laedo, on the contrary, stood his ground as the discarded body of Klystar bore down on him.

'Klystar' halted. "You should not be here," he said curtly. "You are not one of the body servitors."

"*You* should not be here!" Laedo shouted at him. "You are committing atrocities! You are murdering children! So much for your 'superiority'!"

"One might as well listen to the arguments of ants," 'Klystar' retorted, "as to your maundering protests about 'morality'. Your 'ethics' has no objective basis. It is simply a species-survival strategy. Klystar's intelligence, on the other hand, is aligned with objective reality."

His voice rose. "To be the instrument of Klystar is high fortune for one such as you. Go, my friend, and become part of Klystar!"

Without warning the Klystar body lashed out with an arm which was surprisingly strong. Laedo was tumbled and tipped into the nearest vat.

The fleshy odour overwhelmed him. The thick yellow fluid closed over his head. He tried to raise himself, only to discover that there was nothing to push up against. The bottom of the vat lay far below the level of the gallery floor. He realized that the six vats were in fact openings of a single larger tank.

He was sinking, but there was no sense of suffocation. He felt no need to breathe. Neither was there complete darkness: a flesh-coloured glow surrounded him. But there was nothing to see apart from vague shadows which might have been faces, bodies, or anything. What there was, quite distinctly, was flickering presences. Helsey Fong was somewhere nearby, feebly protesting. The process of absorption into the fluid was slow. Individuals briefly and sketchily reconstituted themselves. The pus-like yellow muck was a turmoil of bewildered children—they were mostly children—being mixed together as if in some cooking process.

Laedo made swimming motions in an attempt to reach the surface. It was impossible. The more he struggled, the more the custard of melted life resisted. At length he despaired, and was on the point of letting himself sink to the bottom of the tank, when he felt a hand seize his. A slender hand, without a great deal of strength, but with its aid he was able to break free, pushing upward and lifting his head clear.

To his astonishment he had not been more than a foot or two below the surface all the time. The fluid was somehow able to restrain its victims. But now it let him go. It had no wetness, no ability to cling. Instead it poured from him as he gripped the side of the tank and clambered over it. Not a drop of the flesh-stuff remained on him.

"What happened?" he gasped.

"I hid on the stairs till the monster went," Histrina said in hushed tones. "Since then I've been feeling about in the tank looking for you."

"Thanks."

Laedo embraced Histrina in genuine gratitude.

"Where did he go?"

"Through that door at the other end."

"Let's get away from here."

Like scared mice they scuttled to the stairway.

NINE

The Poisoned Chalice

While running back to the cargo ship Laedo told himself that he might now have an advantage. 'Klystar' would think him absorbed into the life-vat, his substance unwillingly donated to the formation of Klystar's next body.

Once inside the ship's lounge he sat down to think.

Histrina watched him with concern. "What are we going to do?" she asked anxiously.

Laedo didn't answer. Matters were becoming clear in his mind. He had to do more than simply escape, if indeed that was possible at all. It was his duty to oppose Klystar.

He wondered if his cargo carrier's defence blaster would be capable of destroying the main palace, or least that part of it containing the vat. He rejected the idea. He would be firing on innocent people, and besides the palace might well be capable of defending itself.

There might be a sneakier way of foiling Klystar.

Sunset came. All the Erspia worlds had a twenty-eight hour day, but the moon's orbit gave it a much briefer period. Laedo had slept for only a few hours when the artificial sun came up again. He left Histrina fast asleep, and armed with a flashlight, made his way to the *Excelsior*.

He paused, sensing the derelict old starliner all around him. Hull integrity had held and the ship had done its settling long ago. It was eerie to think what it must have been like when in service, thronging with people. Especially weird was to contemplate their fright and bewilderment when the liner was seized by Klystar. As before, Laedo passed through a ballroom, a couple of salons, and descended to the cargo hold where Garo's stasis cabinet rested.

It was many years since he had travelled on a starliner. He was trying to recall the likely layout. Where would the engineering section be?

Once through the other end of the cargo hold all lights were out. Garo was conserving power, lighting only that part of the ship he planned to walk through. Laedo switched on his flashlight. He was heading towards the stern of the ship, where he reckoned the crude mechanics of drive and power would be located. He got early confirmation. The elegance of the passenger section was gone. His flashlight flickered on bare metal and plastic, seams and rivets. Only the crew would come here.

In a ship of this size there must surely be facilities for effecting repairs: a machine shop, in other words. It perplexed him that he had not thought of this before. Another result of his mental confusion, perhaps, though very likely everything in the machine shop was wrecked.

In due course Laedo discovered the engine room. The huge windings of the inertial drive which had once propelled the *Excelsior* at several hundred times the velocity of light were a slumped mass of fused and molten metal.

Several doors led from the engine room. Through one of these Laedo found the machine shop. As anticipated, Klystar had trashed this also. Lathes, mills and forming machines were smashed, knocked over, melted, and even the benches on which they had stood mangled into useless shapes. Laedo passed along two lines of machines, training his flashlight on each machine in turn. When he reached the far extent of the room a faint smile came to his lips. Klystar had not been entirely thorough. Probably he had done no more than aim some type of destructive device from the doorway, because a forming machine at the end of the further row had been torn from its mooring bolts and tumbled to the floor, but remained in one piece.

Laedo knelt to examine it. The data processing unit was smashed, so the machine would have to be set up by hand. Laedo was no kind of engineer, but if he could lug the machine back to his cargo ship, power it up and study it for a while, then *maybe* he could make the part he needed from some piece of metal left lying around.

Maybe.

But that wasn't his immediate concern. In the ruined engine section should be something else useful. Laedo used his nose and followed dead, sterile smells years old. In a darkened, blackened corridor he found what he wanted, still seeping with infinite slowness from ruptured tanks: a thick sludge of oil, toxic metals, and exotic compounds. Another search produced a bucket flung in a corner a century and a half earlier. Laedo scooped up a quantity of the sludge and carried it out of the *Excelsior*.

Treading the yellow moss, he climbed up the declivity until the roofs of the pleasure palaces came in sight. The rest of his plan depended on simple daring. He made the short journey to the main palace, passed through the magnificent entrance, and into the great entrance hall, still carrying the bucket.

Few people were about. Encouraged, Laedo started across the hall. Then he froze as a voice spoke behind him.

"What's that you've got there?"

A young woman in a loose-fitting light green gown was staring at the bucket, her nose wrinkled in distaste. Laedo smiled in embarrassment.

"It's from the food tanks. I'm taking it to reprocessing."

"Oh.

Her face blank with incomprehension, she gave a curt nod and moved on.

Sighing with relief, Laedo continued on to the broad staircase, mounted to the outside balcony, and thence to the narrow corridor and spiral stairs. When nearly at the top he raised his eyes just above floor level and peeped furtively into the gallery.

It was unoccupied.

With alacrity Laedo leaped up the remaining steps, sprang to the nearest vat and upended his bucket. The thick, dark, oily sludge poured with treacly slowness into the pus-coloured fluid. He watched in fascination as it spread and formed tentacles and swirls and multicoloured stains, tainting and poisoning the flesh substance that was meant to form Klystar's new body.

Would 'Klystar', or the team which serviced the tank, discover the pollution? It would be rash to think otherwise, but Laedo paused to consider Klystar's carelessness. There was a singular lack of security—in consequence, perhaps, of Klystar's contempt for human intelligence.

Though still fascinated by the spreading discoloration, which had reached the other openings by now, he decided he had been here long enough. He turned and made for the stairs.

Then the hairs on the back of his neck prickled. There came a slamming sound, together with a rushing, sloshing noise.

He whirled. The oval vats, really openings of a single tank, had slid to the extreme ends of the gallery, revealing the full extent of the ochre slime.

That slime was surging towards the middle of the tank. The air crackled. A dramatic transformation was taking place, a tumultuous rising, a gushing spout which formed itself into a tall figure.

And stepped from the tank.

The figure resembled 'Klystar', complete with the long spindly legs, the four spindly arms and the turreted, swiftly rotating head. But it was much more invigorated, with an integument of brilliant shining yellow in place of the pale pastel of the older body.

Laedo stared, transfixed.

Klystar had returned.

Here at last was the creator of the Erspia worlds: Klystar the ancient, the polymath, who held in a single consciousness more knowledge than was possessed by the whole of mankind.

It was stupefying to think of his achievements. His method of travel meant that he could take no instruments with him, yet unaided he had shaped planetoids, built machines, worked wonders. Such feats were impossible except with the aid of supreme knowledge.

Drops and gobs of life-substance dripped from Klystar as he stood before Laedo, bending his head to regard him. The turret was rotating back and forth with rapidity. The five separately functioning eyes flashed with fiendish intelligence.

Laedo became absolutely certain that here was a being who never slept or rested, and who never paused from ceaseless mentation.

He wished he had brought his gun with him. What subconscious impulse had prompted him to leave it behind? Was it to avoid the possibility, always a horror to him, of having to kill a sentient being while in that being's presence?

Perhaps he had accomplished the act already. Purple discoloration was appearing on Klystar's body, creating a mottling effect. Klystar appeared to flinch. A vibrant voice issued from the turreted head.

"Is it you who has poisoned this body? Everything is dis-

rupted."

A *click* sounded. The tall door through which 'Klystar' had earlier exited opened. The previous body of the polymath strode through, walked a short distance, then stopped, facing its replacement.

Modulated sounds passed between the two: some sort of high-speed language. The newly arrived Klystar sagged and staggered. Its paler, older counterpart started, as if in shock, eyes briefly becoming a thousand times more alive than before, flashing fire. Then, in the same moment that the new Klystar collapsed to the floor, they waned into dullness once more.

"What has happened?" Laedo whimpered.

'Klystar' rotated his head to regard him with a single middle eye. He spoke in a reedy voice which was much weaker than before. "You have successfully sabotaged Klystar's body replacement. It is defunct. He was forced to take refuge in this body temporarily."

"Then do I now address the real Klystar?"

"No, you do not. Klystar lingered only long enough to obtain the Erspia data from me, though he would have preferred to review the results for himself. He has already left for a new destination." With no change of tone, 'Klystar' added, "It may please you to hear that inadvertently you have forestalled the imminent destruction of the specimens. Klystar is meticulous in his actions. He would have closed down the experiment on completion, reducing the Erspia worlds to the rubble from which they were formed."

To realize that he had emptied his bucket into the tank in the nick of time gave Laedo a sense of destiny. "Then will you do that yourself? Or continue in charge as before?"

"I am unable to do either. You have killed not only the new body, but the old one as well. In a few minutes both will lie dead on the floor of this chamber."

"I don't understand," puzzled Laedo.

"It is simple enough. Immediacy of Thought is like stretching a piece of elastic and letting one end go. It snaps forward and stings the fingers. The longer the stretch, the greater the violence of contraction. A transfer from galaxy to galaxy delivers a shock so great it is lethal to an aged body such as speaks to you now."

"But that doesn't make sense," protested Laedo. "You did not receive Klystar from another galaxy, only from across the room!"

'Klystar' made no immediate answer. He appeared to be gathering his remaining strength. When he responded, it was in a dry voice. "Are you hungry for knowledge, or merely argumentative?" Again his head rotated slowly, dim eyes staring in turn. "Immediacy of Thought, though described as instantaneous, in practice takes several minutes to accomplish in full. The essence of the traveller is projected in a wave train stretching the length of the distance to be traversed. That is the 'elastic band'. It is the leading end which makes instant contact with the target. The rear end is then released, and the wave train contracts into its new location in a non-zero time interval. The Klystar who spoke to you was not the whole Klystar but a partial representation, the vanguard of the wave train. On finding that the new body was poisoned he switched the target to me in order to collect the Erspia data. I-Klystar received the full force of the remaining wave train."

Now Laedo understood. He had frustrated Klystar, denying him a receptacle. The polymath had been forced to depart and could not have remained. It was to be hoped he had no further reason to return.

'Klystar's' voice was growing weaker. He slumped. The lack of rancour on his part was a striking element. Laedo had wreaked considerable inconvenience on Klystar, yet there was no hint of seeking revenge. And why should there be? Such attitudes were part of the social dimension, which in Klystar was absent.

Also curious was the readiness to spend one's last moments explaining technical matters to a near-stranger and proven enemy. It was the dying reflex of one dominated by the compulsive hunt for knowledge.

The next words, however, were far from reassuring. "It took Klystar only seconds to evaluate the data and render a judgment. It is this. Your species is unstable in evolutionary terms. Its survival index is low. True intelligence will begin its appearance in this galaxy in about two billion years time. Klystar may well be still alive then. But *homo sapiens*, as you term yourselves, will have devolved back to the simian level in less then half a million years from now, your spurious intelligence evaporated . . ."

'Klystar' was losing his ability to stand upright. Slowly he toppled. As he lay on the floor Laedo made a hurried, if impudent, request.

"Can you release control of the projector station to me?"

'Klystar' was still. *"Projector station . . ."* he whispered. And then was silent.

Laedo stepped to the inert body and kicked it. "Speak!"

There was no response.

At the other end of the gallery the extra-tall door clicked open. Half a dozen men and women, all clad the same, in loose blue trousers and blouses patterned in silver-and-gold, entered. On seeing the two dead Klystar bodies they halted.

"What has happened?"

The shocked question came from a man somewhat older than the others, with streaks of grey in his hair.

These would be the body servitors referred to by 'Klystar', a team charged with maintaining the flesh tank.

"Klystar has returned, and gone away again," Laedo announced. "You can close the project down now. He will not return a second time. The tank needs no more victims."

Ignoring their stunned looks, he left the gallery. No one tried to stop him as he descended the spiral stairs, regained the grand entrance hall and walked back to his cargo ship, where he found Histrina stirring into wakefulness. He told her to get herself some breakfast, then made his way once more to the *Excelsior*. It took him more than an hour to lug the damaged forming machine to his own ship and place it in storage there. Then he made one more trip, searching till he found several pieces of metal which he hoped were of the right quality. These also he stored.

By then Histrina had eaten a plate of pancakes. She gave him some coffee, which he gulped gratefully.

He looked at her with a new sense of pity. If he was any judge, a rude awakening was in store for her.

On the external viewscreen he saw that a large body of people had emerged from the palace complex and was marching on the cargo ship. The palace staff had finally got their wits together and were in a mood to ask questions.

"Time we were going, Histrina."

He powered the manoeuvring engine. The ship soared above the small moonscape, leaving the approaching crowd gawping.

The atmosphere ended abruptly five miles up. It took only a short while to cross space to the atmosphere of Erspia-5. Laedo eased the ship into it and began to look for the grounded projector station among the spread of fields and villages.

That took a little longer, but eventually he spotted the spherical shape. Hovering briefly to unlock its portal with a radio burst, he settled beside it, to see that men were working in the nearby field as before.

Already they were running towards the ship. Brio Fong was among them. Reluctantly Laedo rose from the control panel and took himself outside.

Anxiously Brio searched his face. He pointed a finger at the sky.

"Have you been—up there? To the Heavenly Mansion?"

Poker-faced, Laedo nodded.

"Did you see my little Helsey?" Brio asked eagerly. "Is she happy?"

Laedo stayed poker-faced. "No," he lied, "I didn't see her."

He turned away to face the projector station. The radio burst had not only released the lock on the portal but had also brought the access stairway snaking down to the ground. That had not happened when he had used the same trick in space. He thought only the lever Histrina had found worked that mechanism. Anyway, it saved him the trouble of having to climb up to the entrance by means of treads and handgrips on the station's outer skin.

Histrina had appeared at the doorway. He beckoned her on to the turf, locked the door, then led her into the projector station, ignoring the Erspians altogether.

He seated himself at the control board and spoke into the air.

"The experiment is complete. Klystar has gathered his data and departed. Pass control of this station to me."

The printer chattered, ejecting a sheet of parchment through the slot.

Completion confirmed. Control transferred to manual or

voice.

It was hardly likely that the mechanism was taking his word for it. Laedo deduced that 'Klystar' had ordered the station to relinquish control, as requested, in his last moments.

Surprisingly, there was a civilised side to Klystar's bodily shell after all.

He sat there thinking. The sensible thing now would be to affix his cargo ship to its previous pick-a-back position on the station, and set course for Harkio. If, that was, the projector station staff had been told the truth by Klystar.

Laedo saw no reason to believe that.

And anyway Laedo was no longer thinking sensibly. Incongruously acting as his conscience, 'Klystar' had made him aware of a wrong he had committed, and which he had to make amends for, inasmuch as that was possible. Furthermore it had to be done without delay, for delay would be unethical. He could not merely fly to Harkio and then try to direct the help of the authorities from there.

What he planned would jeopardise his original mission, true. But there was no other course.

He turned to Histrina. "How would you like to visit your home village?"

She clapped her hands. "Oh yes! I can see my family!"

Leaving his seat, he took Histrina's hands in his.

"Do you still feel that you belong to Ahriman?"

Frowning, she shook her heed. "I can't say I feel I belong to anyone or anything."

"But Ahriman rules on your world. The goodness of Ormazd has been taken away. Hoggora has had plenty of time to reach your village. Everyone there might be dead."

Histrina, of course, did not know what he was talking about; did not know what he had done and probably would not be able to understand it, despite his earlier effort to explain the artificial nature of the twin gods.

She shook her head again, more vigorously then before. "Oh no! There is an army to keep the evil ones at bay. Hoggora's camp was fun . . . but he'll never get through to Courhart."

"Things may be different now, Histrina," Laedo said sadly.

He spoke to the control board. "Show me a map of the Erspia worlds."

The panel obeyed. A hitherto blank extra viewplate displayed an ebony background against which glowed a number of locations connected by lines on which distances were printed.

There were in fact twelve Erspias, not ten as Garo had thought. But which was which? Though he had privately numbered those he had visited One to Five, he didn't know if there was an actual numbering. The locations on the screen had neither numbers nor names.

He spoke again.

"Return the Ormazd projector to its original position."

At once he heard the whine of the main drive starting up. The station swayed and lifted into the air. In hardly more than seconds they were again in the blackness of space, hurtling through the cluster of worldlets.

Two plans of action had occurred to Laedo. One was to park his cargo ship on the projector station, pick-a-back, as before, return the projector station to its proper place, and switch the Ormazd beam back on, thus restoring the *status quo ante*. He could then set about trying to make a transductor, and if successful, go home.

But he wasn't satisfied with the *status quo ante*. He wanted to free the Erspians from mind control altogether. So he had decided on his second plan, which called for something more drastic. It would also endanger the cargo ship, which was why he had taken the dreadful risk of leaving it behind.

In little more than half an hour a glowing Erspian world swam into view. The station took up its fixed non-orbiting position diametrically opposite the Ahrimanic projector and automatically pointed the projector tube at the planetoid's surface. Nothing issued from it, of course. The beam was still switched off.

Laedo took over the manual controls. He moved the station again, steering it to the other side of the worldlet. Gleaming in the light of the tiny sun, the Ahrimanic globe was wickedly on station.

"See that, Histrina? That's Ahriman's mouth. That's where all your evil thoughts come from. Do you remember my showing it to you before?"

"It's all vague," she murmured, standing behind him. "What are you going to do?"

He waved to her. "Strap yourself into that couch. The inertial field should protect us, but it might get a little bumpy."

He took the station further out and positioned it behind the Ahrimanic globe, which he could see hovering against the beautiful, slowly turning spectacle of Erspia-1. The projector stations did not need to orbit or maintain themselves against Erspia-1's gravity—that petered out some miles below them. Laedo reasoned that the adjusting mechanism which rectified drift would therefore be low-powered. He was gambling that a sudden displacement would be too much for that mechanism to handle.

At a velocity of fifty miles per hour he steered the Ormazdian globe directly at its Ahrimanic twin. It was frightening to see the other projector station expand swiftly on the viewscreen until its striated surface hurtled close and still loomed larger. Histrina screamed, her hand to her mouth. Collision came with a shattering, clanging noise which rang throughout the station, but there was little effect on the two humans otherwise—the inertial field ensured that. Instead of being smashed against the forward wall, they felt no more than a shudder. Laedo heard a hiss of escaping air, but he didn't worry about it very much. The inertial field would also be capable of compensating for breaches in hull integrity; if that failed bulkheads would close, sealing off the damaged area.

Ahriman moved, pushed off position. Where the two globes came in contact they seemed stuck together, but this was only because Laedo was keeping up the pressure, accelerating Ahriman down towards the surface of Erspia-1.

As soon as they hit the atmosphere he disengaged. Ahriman kept on falling, well within the gravity well by now. If the station staff, demented as they would be by a century and a half of living in the backwash of the evil beam, still had the presence of mind to activate the star drive, then his gamble would be lost.

He had been careful not to take Histrina and himself through the Ahrimanic beam. He continued to stay well clear of it as he followed the station down, aware that the structure might start to tumble. It did not appear to recover, but plummeted towards the ground, hurtling through the thin cloud layer.

At the very end the staff seemed to make some attempt to regain control. The station faltered in its trajectory. But it was too late. The globe struck the ground and crumpled, then went rolling much as the Ormazdian station had on Erspia-2, though with far more destructive results. When it came to rest, it was all but shattered. As for the cylindrical tube of the beam projector, that was gone altogether, the place where it had been gaping up at the sky.

Very likely the staff had survived. The inertial field should have held through all or most of the landing, which would have saved them.

But with luck, the station itself was permanently out of action. Dipping low, he passed several times over the wreck to test whether any violent thoughts came into his mind. He detected nothing abnormal.

Erspia-1's long, artificially contrived moral drama was over.

Turning the station aside, he began, with Histrina's help, to search for the village of Courhart.

TEN

Homecoming

Histrina's heart was in her mouth as they sailed through the air over her home world. Her mind was in confusion. She could remember doing violent things, even killing people, but it was as if somebody else had done them. She could not, now, understand what had made her behave in that way.

She was nervous of coming home. She was *extremely* nervous of facing the priest and confessing her sins. But she was also eager to see her family again. She felt as though she had been away for years, though in reality it was only days.

After a while she spotted a landmark: a range of high hills known as the Thespan Mounts. Laedo had noticed that similar formations dotted all the Erspia worlds. He surmised that Klystar had put them there as windbreaks; part of a pattern of climatic variation.

They passed over the smashed and still-smoking remains of villages. Once they saw a column of men, some mounted, some on foot, dragging themselves towards an unknown destination. The men gawped upwards as the projector station passed over, momentarily pausing from their incessant quarrels and fights. Their once gaudy apparel was bedraggled and torn.

Histrina became more and more frightened as she saw the burned and deserted villages. When Courhart came in sight she shrieked.

It was the same as everywhere else. The roofs of the few unburnt cottages had been stoved in. But unlike in many of the other villages, there were still some people about, stumbling among the ruins.

And what gave her some faint cause for hope, the chapel still stood.

Knuckles in her mouth, she sat staring at the screen. Guided by Laedo, the station descended and set down outside the village.

He turned to her, and said gently, "I told you there might be bad news, Histrina."

Histrina gave a bird-like cry and ran from the control room along the corridor leading to the hatch. Before Laedo could gather his wits she had pulled the lever to open it and was hurrying down the stairway even as it unfolded. She went racing towards the ruined village.

What a terrible sight! Blackened walls, desolation, smashed furniture thrown out into the streets. Histrina looked wildly about her for some sign of life. She spotted a ragged boy sitting on a wall, head hanging. She ran up to him. He raised a smudged, tear-stained face. Even in his wretched condition she recognised him.

"Tippy!"

In place of a greeting, the youngster gave her an evil leer.

Then his face collapsed and he began to weep in snivelling sobs.

Her home! Histrina left the boy and ran until she came to the cottage where she had been raised.

It had been burned like the others.

Disconsolately she wandered through the charred, once cosy rooms. Where were her parents? Where was her younger sister Questra? There was no sign of them.

The sound of footsteps brought her to the door. Ragged, bearded, weaponed men stood grinning at her. From their colourful clothing she knew they were of Hoggora's camp; but they seemed to have forgotten to take care of their appearance. It was as if they were too sunk in depravity to care. Indeed they seemed exhausted.

"What a choice morsel," said one teasingly. He grinned, showing white teeth. "How about it, lads?"

Another spoke sullenly. "Hoggora says the young ones are to be taken to the chapel, for the Father."

"Oh, for the Father." The first speaker shrugged, and turned away. "Take her, then."

The Father! Perhaps he could tell her if her family was safe! Unresistingly Histrina allowed herself to be grabbed by the wrist and led away. At the entrance porch to the chapel, she was yanked roughly within.

It was as she remembered. The coolness, the sense of calm,

the slanting sunlight penetrating the dimness.

But something was wrong. Instead of the aroma of incense, there was the smell of blood.

"More sport for you, Father," said the warrior who had brought her here. "We found her in one of the cottages."

He departed. Histrina directed her gaze down the length of the chapel.

The priest of the Good God, Father Gromund whom she had known all her life, was standing by the alter. As usual he was dressed in his brocaded robe with the golden sunburst on the front. But his hair was matted and tangled, and the robe itself was stained and dirtied.

Dirtied. With dried blood.

Father Gromund turned to meet her gaze. His eyes widened in recognition.

"Histrina! My dear young Histrina! I have you at last!" he made an impatient gesture into the shadows. *"Bring her here!"*

Father Gromund's tonsured acolyte crept forward into the sunlight. Whereas before his young face had been soft, doe-eyed, almost effeminate, now it was grim and determined. He quickened his pace, strode to Histrina and grabbed her roughly by the arm. "Come."

Dragging her the length of the nave, he thrust her at the priest and disappeared once more into the darkness.

Then Histrina's bewilderment began in earnest. Before she knew what was happening Father Gromund had picked her up and had lain her back on the altar. Expertly he fastened thongs to her wrists and ankles. These were fixed to the altar in some way. She was helpless, lying face up, arms and legs drawn down to the floor.

"Father! What are you doing?"

"What I have always wanted to do, my child." Father Gromund's voice was unctuous and gloating. "Oh, to have been entrusted with the morals of so many sweet young things, to have heard every intimate confession, to have known every dirty thought—and *finally!"*

He ripped open her lower garments and worked his fingers enthusiastically in her sexual cleft.

"You are a priest of Ormazd!" she protested hysterically.

"Ormazd has deserted this world, child. Ahriman triumphs, and I am *his* priest now. It is so much more fun, after all! I have enjoyed your mother, and your sister, and now, sweetest of all, there is you, dear desirable Histrina. Do you wish to see your sister? Look over there. See what is in store for you."

Histrina turned her head to follow his pointing finger. There, lying in shadow before the pews, was the naked body of her sister Questra. It bore countless ugly wounds and gashes. Questra had been beheaded, the head laid carefully beside the severed neck. Even in death her faced grimaced with indescribable suffering.

And nearby, on a low table, were the instruments which had been used on her. Knives, gimlets, a large axe. All were encrusted with blood.

In sheer grief, Histrina shrieked. The priest leaned over her, bringing his face close to hers. His eyes were shining. "I do not expect you to understand, my dear," he said, looking into her horrified, staring eyes. "It takes one of education, such as I. You see, in obedience to Ormazd we had to repress so much. Everything had to be dammed up. Now the dam has burst, releasing *a madness of lechery and torture.*"

With the last words he drew himself erect, lifting his face and raising his hands in the air, his voice wavering on the edge of sanity like a bird attempting to soar beyond the atmosphere. Then he regarded her again.

"Let it begin!"

He pulled up his robe. His penis was a ramrod in his hand. Guiding it to her vagina, he thrust it home. Then he was bucking against her, lips drawn back, grunting and growling.

And Histrina sobbed and sobbed.

Standing on the platform atop the steps of the station, Laedo soon lost sight of Histrina among the ruined cottages. He sighed with frustration. A fair number of armed men roamed the village.

He set off after her, but had not reached the first row of houses when a party of nearly a dozen warriors emerged to charge at him, waving swords and shouting incoherently. One hurled a spear which narrowly missed him. He drew his gun and got off a couple of shots, aiming at his attackers' legs and bringing one of them down.

He could probably have killed all dozen if he chose—but could he kill all of Hoggora's men in the village? And what would be happening to Histrina meanwhile? He retreated back to the station and pulled the steps up after him.

There was another, different weapon. A weapon of pure goodness.

Seated before the console in the control room, he lifted the lid of the sturdy box bolted to the board. Within was the lever with which he had switched off the Ormazdian beam.

Laedo seized the lever in his right hand, and pushed. The lever clunked to ON.

He energised the engine with a trickle of power. The station rose a hundred feet in the air. Nudging the directional knobs, he pointed the projector tube at the ground. Then he steered it to hover over the village.

Nothing on the console told him whether the beam was actually working. The projector could have been damaged when the station made its crash landing on Erspia-2. But assuming that it was, then Courhart was now receiving, at full intensity, a beam strength initially designed to spread out and cover the entire planetoid.

Offhand, he was unable to calculate what the spread would be at only a hundred feet. To make sure he criss-crossed the village, hoping to invade all the dwellings below with concentrated waves of pure goodness.

Arrows and slingshot stones rattled against the underside of the station. Laedo bit his lip. Perhaps the beam was defunct after all. He considered setting the station down on the village and crushing what was left of the buildings here and there, cowing the occupiers by sheer bulk and force.

Then, through the viewscreen, he saw men drop their weapons and fall to their knees. Their hands were clasped together, their faces raised, their mouths working in anguished prayer.

He was seeing human beings turn from evil to good by the application of a piece of technology.

It would be easy to be cynical. Maybe Klystar was right.

He wondered how Histrina was getting on.

Father Gromund had raped her, had urinated all over her, had hit her full in the face with his fist, and now was selecting an instrument with which, just as an *hors d'oeuvre*, to cut off her right breast.

He let her see the knife, turning it so that the filtered sunlight gleamed on the blade, singing to it in a soft crooning voice, enjoying the look of stark terror on her bruised and bloody face.

Then the beam hit. His mind became full of confusion. The knife fell from his fingers and rang on the floor.

Histrina felt it too. It was like a pure white light shining through her brain, washing away every wicked thought, bringing back the innocence of her childhood. Her upbringing came back to her in full flood. Feelings of benevolence filled her. Looking at the triumph of evil that surrounded her, she felt even greater horror, suffused with pity.

Father Gromund, too, was looking about him in stupefaction. His eyes boggled in disbelief as he beheld the mutilated corpse of poor Questra, realizing that he himself had been the jubilant perpetrator of her gruesome death. He threw himself at Histrina's bonds, freeing her and helping her to her feet.

He fell to his knees.

"My child, my child! What have I done? Oh, Ormazd!"

Snatching up the knife, he offered it to her handle first.

"Take your revenge on me! Plunge the knife into my heart!"

Histrina took it from him, but flung it aside. She too fell to her knees. "What have *I* done, Father? I have killed people! I have soiled my virtue! And I don't know why!"

Sobbing together, clutching one another, they both called piteously on Ormazd for forgiveness.

Histrina wore a simple white dress reaching to her ankles. A white flower was in her hair. On her face was a permanent look of sorrow.

She was looking down on Erspia-1 through the viewscreen. At first, when Laedo came for her, she had wanted to stay in Courhart. True, most of the people she had grown up with were dead, including her immediate family, but it was her home.

Laedo had dissuaded her. He felt it his duty to take her to Harkio, for treatment from his personal mentalist. Besides, she had been through enough, and life was going to be uncertain on Erspia-1 from now on.

He had done the best he could. He had taken the station up into space, choosing a midway elevation where the effects of the Ormazd beam would still be somewhat stronger than from its original height, and he had criss-crossed the planetoid, just as he had the village of Courhart, making sure that its influence would reach everywhere.

Then, when he judged the Ahrimanic influence had been counterbalanced, he had switched the beam off for good. The people of Erspia-1 were now free from artificial mental influence. They could work out their own attitudes, find their own consciences.

If there was such a thing as conscience.

Even then, it would take some time.

When he made his report to the authorities, they would feel it their duty to send help to the twelve Erspia worlds. That would present problems, quite apart from the considerable expense. He did not know, for instance how assistance could be rendered to the genetically altered fairies and gnomes of the split planetoid.

But there would be a pay-back, in the acquisition of Klystar technology, particularly the thought beams.

Which could, of course, be used for either good or ill, but mostly for ill. Perhaps the technique would be banned, buried, deemed too dangerous to human freedom.

"Are we going to Harkio now?" Histrina asked.

Laedo shook his heed. "Not straight away. I don't trust this heap of cobbled-together junk to get us there. We're going back to my cargo ship. I'm going to see if I can make a transductor."

Good and bad. That was the difference.

Laedo took his eyes off the human nest that was the Erspian worldlet. He thought of the great swirling Milky Way galaxy, fermenting with life.

"Ants," he muttered. "He called us ants."

Ants. But there was a difference, after all. Klystar had drawn on human religious ideas in designing the two thought projectors. But he himself had no preference between the two, either for Ormazd or for Ahriman. No choice between good and evil—for him, neither existed. He was pure intellect, pure curiosity, an ethical nullity, oblivious of the impact his actions had on others.

Which in human terms, was one way of defining a psychopath.

An entire cosmic generation of sentient beings had arisen blind to the drama of Ormazd and Ahriman.

Man could choose between them. Of course, it remained true what Klystar had said. Human consciousness was feeble and deluded, ludicrously prone to being swayed by persuasion, when compared with the shining, unassailable consciousness of Klystar.

But unlike Klystar's, mankind's evolution was not yet over.

Still mulling over the conundrum, Laedo steered the projector station back towards Erspia-5.

www.ingramcontent.com/pod-product-compliance
Lightning Source LLC
Chambersburg PA
CBHW020334260626
47156CB00004B/1515